Murd

in

Room 346

Phillip Strang

BOOKS BY PHILLIP STRANG

DCI Isaac Cook Series
MURDER IS A TRICKY BUSINESS
MURDER HOUSE
MURDER IS ONLY A NUMBER
MURDER IN LITTLE VENICE
MURDER IS THE ONLY OPTION
MURDER IN NOTTING HILL
MURDER IN ROOM 346
MURDER WITHOUT REASON

DI Keith Tremayne Series
DEATH UNHOLY
DEATH AND THE ASSASSIN'S BLADE
DEATH AND THE LUCKY MAN

Steve Case Series
HOSTAGE OF ISLAM
THE HABERMAN VIRUS
PRELUDE TO WAR

Standalone Books
MALIKA'S REVENGE

Copyright Page

Dedication

For Elli and Tais who both had the perseverance to make me sit down and write.

Chapter 1

'Coitus interruptus, that's what it is,' Detective Chief Inspector Isaac Cook said. It was to be the only attempt at humour that day, and even then, it was in bad taste. On the bed, in a downmarket hotel in Bayswater, lay the naked bodies of a man and a woman.

'Bullet in the head's not the way to go,' Larry Hill, Isaac Cook's detective inspector, said. He had not expected such a flippant comment from his senior, not when they were standing near to two people who had, apparently in the final throes of passion, succumbed to what appeared to be a professional assassination.

'Do you recognise him?'

'James Holden, from what I can see.'

'And the woman?'

'According to the driving licence in her purse, her name was Helen Langdon. There's an address in Kensington, good street.'

'Judging by her clothes, she had plenty of money.'

'An attractive woman, or at least, she was.'

Isaac Cook could understand what his DI meant. The woman was not so attractive sprawled across the bed, the blood congealing on her and the sheets.

'No idea what she saw in him,' Larry said.

'Rent by the hour?'

'Not according to her handbag. There's a business card. She worked for the man.'

Gordon Windsor, the crime scene examiner, came over. 'Apart from you two talking while I'm trying to focus, I'll give you what I've found so far.'

'You know this will be all over the media within the hour,' Isaac said.

'James Holden, moral crusader, a proponent of the sanctity of the marital bed, man and wife. It's bound to be.'

'The man preaches one thing, practises another.'

'They've all got hidden secrets. Anyway, this is what we have,' Windsor said. 'Helen Langdon, age thirty-two, James Holden, age seventy-two. Both have been shot in the head.'

'Whoever did this knew what they were doing,' Larry said. 'Somehow the person managed to get into the room unseen, and then get close enough to the pair to hold the gun to each of their heads.'

'They were occupied, maybe they didn't look,' Isaac said.

'We'll check, but it's clear that they were indulging in sexual intercourse.'

'The man was seventy-two,' Isaac said.

'It's alright for you young studs,' Windsor said, 'but let me tell you, life is not over at fifty.'

'But James Holden was not fit, and he was always preaching against this sort of thing,' Larry said.

'I can only give you the facts,' Windsor said. 'Why the man was here with a young woman is for you to find out. And why he was killed, that's up to you. Their bodies will be with Pathology later today. I suggest you ask there in a day or so for any more information, but they'll only confirm what I've just said.'

Isaac knew that Windsor was correct in his evaluation. They had known each other for many years, he, the first-generation English-born son of Jamaican parents, and Gordon Windsor, the smallish, rotund man in his late fifties.

Back in the office at Challis Street Police Station, Sergeant Wendy Gladstone, the best person if you needed to find

2

someone, and Bridget Halloran, who ran the office, would already be preparing the case for the prosecution.

Wendy and Bridget were firm friends, sharing a house since Wendy's husband had died and Bridget had kicked out her layabout live-in lover.

DI Larry Hill maintained an uneasy truce with his wife and her faddish diets, but he was looking a lot better since she and his DCI had ganged up on him to moderate his food intake and the pints of beer.

The only thorn in the side of the Homicide department was Seth Caddick, a man who had once temporarily occupied Isaac's seat as the senior investigating officer in Homicide, only to be unceremoniously eased out after Isaac had solved the case, but now he was back, and this time as his senior. The sycophantic, and to Isaac incompetent, Caddick had somehow managed to attain the rank of Detective Superintendent, and he was in Detective Chief Superintendent Richard Goddard's office, and he was in charge.

Isaac Cook had respected Goddard, a man who had got on the wrong side of the London Metropolitan Police commissioner, Alwyn Davies. Caddick, a man who for some reason always came up smelling of roses, had been quick to claim it was his leadership that ensured the enviable success rate of the Homicide department, when it was clearly Isaac and his team.

Not that it concerned Isaac unduly, as Goddard had explained that Caddick's tenure was to be short-lived, but it was already five months, and the man continued to irritate and interfere.

***

Back in the office at Challis Street, Isaac gathered the team. He had phoned Caddick out of courtesy, knowing the man's reaction if was ignored. Isaac had come close to insubordination on a couple of occasions, and Goddard, his former senior, had told him to play the game and not to rile the man.

Isaac wasn't sure how much longer he could put up with Caddick. The man continued to be a mediocre performer, and morale was down, with a few people transferring out of Challis Street, some others just resigning. So far, none of Isaac's core team had left, and he was hopeful he could keep it that way.

'Bridget, what do we have?' Isaac asked. The woman was computer-savvy, and she could find out things about a person that no one else could.

'James Aloysius Holden, age seventy-two, married to Violet Holden, two children. John, age thirty-seven, a lawyer. His sister, Linda, age thirty-three, a social worker.'

'Helen Langdon was younger than his daughter,' Larry said.

'It sounds indecent to me,' Wendy said.

'Bridget, carry on. We can discuss the age difference afterwards.'

'James Holden, Member of Parliament, self-professed moral crusader, a staunch advocate for prison reform and controls on the internet. And also, a believer in one man, one woman, and total fidelity.'

'Not practising what he preaches,' Larry said.

'They're all the same,' Wendy said. She was in her fifties, troubled with arthritis, and putting on weight after giving up a lifetime habit of smoking. She was not an admirer of those born with a silver spoon in their mouth, or the hypocrites in society who preach one thing, do another.

'Not all,' Isaac said, 'but in this case, there's some explaining to do. What do we know about his wife?'

'She's been notified,' Bridget said.

'Wendy, it may be best if you come with me. Do we have her address?' Isaac said.

'Ebury Street, Belgravia. We can be there in twenty-five minutes.'

As Isaac and Wendy were preparing to leave, in walked their superintendent, Seth Caddick. 'Where are you off to?' he said.

'We're going to interview the dead man's wife,' Isaac replied.

'Very well. Keep me updated, and make sure your report is in on time.'

Caddick walked out of the office. Larry turned to Isaac. 'How can you put up with him, guv?' he said.

'Play the game, play the game,' Isaac said. 'The man's only keeping the seat warm.'

'For you?'

'That's the word,' Isaac replied with a wry smile.

'And who'll run Homicide?'

'Are you up to it?'

'I reckon so. I just need to pass one more exam, and then I'll be looking for a promotion.'

'As long as you stay with Homicide.'

'My wife's not so keen, not after the time I ended up in the hospital courtesy of a local gang.'

'That can happen walking down the street,' Isaac said, realising that it wasn't entirely accurate. The only reason Larry had not died was due to the ineptitude of his assailants. He had been interviewing a homeless man who had witnessed a murder. His attackers had subsequently dealt with the witness with a knife in the heart.

After the short discussion with Larry, Isaac and Wendy drove out to Ebury Street. 'Nice houses,' Isaac said.

'Out of my budget,' Wendy replied. She feigned disinterest, although Isaac knew she appreciated the beauty of the buildings.

Outside the Holden home, an elegant three-storey, late Georgian, white-painted house, a uniform stood. 'The media has been around. I'm here to deter anyone knocking on the door,' he said. Wendy could tell that he would have preferred to have been anywhere else than at the door of a moral crusader's home, as it was cold and raining, not an unusual occurrence for the time of year.

From inside the house, the door was opened by a man in his thirties. 'My mother is resting,' he said.

Ushered into a room on the left of the hallway, the two police officers waited. A woman entered and placed a tray on the table in front of where they sat. 'Madam will be here soon. The tea's freshly brewed,' she said before leaving.

Violet Holden entered the room. She was helped by John Holden, her son. 'It's come as a great shock to my mother, to all of us,' he said. He was a man of about medium height, his hair cut short, his fingernails manicured, his suit of the best quality.

'Thank you for coming,' Violet Holden said.

'I'm sorry that it's under such circumstances.'

'Is it true what they're reporting?' the woman asked. 'We'd been married for over forty years. I thought I knew the man, and this has come as a shock.'

'His death?'

'I assumed he'd die in the Houses of Parliament, or in some committee or other, even in one of those prisons he frequented, but they're reporting that he was found in bed with another woman. Was it Helen?'

'Helen Langdon. Yes, it was. What can you tell me about her, about your husband?'

'My husband was a saint. It must have been her.'

'Can we come back to your husband,' Isaac said. Holden's wife was taking it badly, but he wasn't sure if it was because of her husband's murder or his adultery.

'What do you want me to tell you? He can't have been with that woman willingly.'

'Unfortunately, there's no question that he was.'

'Is this necessary? My mother is under a great deal of strain,' John Holden said.

'If Mrs Holden is up to it, we should continue,' Isaac said.

Violet Holden patted her son on the arm. 'I'll be fine,' she said.

'Your husband was at a hotel in Bayswater. Do you know of any reason why he would choose there?'

'To be with Helen?'

'Yes.'

'We had advised our father about employing her, but he wouldn't listen,' John Holden said.

'Why?'

'Our father was a great believer in the rehabilitation of criminals after they had served their sentences. Helen had spent time in prison.'

Isaac turned to Wendy. 'Bridget missed that,' he said quietly, ensuring that no one else heard.

'Her name in prison was Helen Mackay.'

'*The* Helen Mackay!'

'She changed her name on leaving prison at my father's suggestion.'

'And your father was part of the rehabilitation process?'

'She was released due to him.'

'Have you met her?' Wendy asked.

'On several occasions. She was pleasant and respectful, devoted to James,' Violet said. 'And now my husband's association with her has got him killed.'

'Until you mentioned her name, we had assumed the reason for their deaths was your husband,' Isaac said.

'Who would have wanted to kill my husband?'

'He must have made powerful enemies. His attempts at censorship must have raised the hackles of a few.'

'My husband wasn't an idealistic bigot. He was a man who had a strong conviction of what was right and wrong.'

'And he's strayed,' Isaac said.

'My husband was a complex man. There were times when his moral crusade became too much for him. Times when he needed to let off steam.'

'This is not the first time?'

'It's the first time with a woman. Sometimes he wanted to come home, put his feet up, have a drink of something strong.'

'Mother, I don't think you should be saying this,' her son said.

'Why not? They're police officers, and they need to know certain facts. And what does it matter? Your father, my husband, has been caught in bed with another woman, and not only that, with Helen Mackay. How do you think your father's legacy is going to stand up when it's revealed that he's been caught in flagrante delicto with a woman who bashed her elderly husband to death with a hammer?'

'Her defence argued it was self-defence, mitigating circumstances,' Isaac said.

'Did anyone believe her when she said she had married for love?' Violet Holden said.

'Did you?' Isaac said.

'Nobody did. Her husband was wealthy, old, and likely to die at any time, and there in the court was a woman in her twenties with a dubious past. The popular press had condemned her the moment she entered the court.'

'The judge believed her. That's why she only received seven years.'

'Out in four. My husband believed in her as well, and then she slept with him, destroying his reputation.'

'Mrs Holden, you don't believe that your husband was coerced, do you?'

'My husband was the same as any other man. Underneath that exterior there was a man of flesh and blood. A man who liked the occasional drink, the occasional woman, the occasional sin.'

'Was this the first time?'

'With Helen, yes.'

'With others?'

'I never knew, although I suspected he did from time to time.'

'Mother, you're maligning my father.'

'Don't pretend, John. You knew what he was like, the same as you.'

Chapter 2

'Moral crusader, serial philanderer, is that what we've got here?' Larry Hill said. The team were back in Homicide at Challis Street Police Station. Thankfully, Detective Superintendent Seth Caddick was not in the building; he was at his favourite place, Scotland Yard, pressing the flesh of whoever he could find, especially Commissioner Alwyn Davies.

Isaac Cook, once seen as an example of the modern police force, knew his star was not shining brightly with the commissioner. When it had been Commissioner Shaw in charge of the London Metropolitan Police, and Richard Goddard his chief superintendent, Isaac's moves on the promotion ladder seemed fine, but he and Goddard had languished under Davies, and Isaac was still a DCI and Goddard had been sidelined into Public Relations.

The problem with Alwyn Davies, according to Isaac and Goddard, was that the man was an incompetent who surrounded himself with other incompetents. There were others, Detective Superintendent Seth Caddick included, who believed that Davies was a man who recognised true ability. It was an impossible situation, Isaac knew, and he had put up with Caddick for almost half a year, and he intended to see the demise of the man's career. The only problem was that as the Homicide team succeeded, so did Caddick, and the man was not slow in pointing it out.

The one skill that Caddick had, apart from irritating Isaac, was that he was an accomplished public speaker. At the wrap-up press conference after someone had been charged with murder, Caddick was able to give the impression that he had single-handedly solved the crime, with Isaac and his team mere functionaries following instructions.

Richard Goddard had been willing to acknowledge his team's contribution, but in front of a microphone and a camera the man was a wet blanket. It had been Isaac who had saved him on several occasions from the ignominy of saying something silly and fluffing his speech. Caddick didn't need any such help, although the interviewers invariably wanted to hear from the tall, good-looking and very dark DCI, not from a dishevelled-looking man with a Welsh accent.

'What do we have on James Holden?' Isaac asked his team. The initial research from Bridget Halloran in the office had been precise, but nothing of a surprise, as the man was well known to the general public.

'Apart from the fact that he was seventy-two with a wife and two children?' Bridget said.

'We need something more than that.'

'James Holden was elected to parliament thirty-three years ago. He held the post of Minister of Health in a previous government, but currently is in opposition.'

'Not much chance of their being returned to power anytime soon,' Wendy Gladstone said.

'Regardless of his party's electoral prospects,' Isaac said.

'James Holden took up the cause of declining moral standards eight years ago,' Bridget continued. 'He's stated on many occasions, passionately in the Houses of Parliament, that more should be done to encourage the institution of marriage, and that graphic violence and sex on the internet and the television are detrimental to society. In the last few years, he's taken on prison reform. According to him, prison is there for rehabilitation, not just for punishment. Holden has made an effort to take recently released prisoners who showed remorse for their crimes and to find them suitable employment, not a dead-end job paying the minimum wage.'

'Helen Langdon, is she one of these prisoners?' Isaac asked.

'Helen Langdon, previously known as Helen Mackay, had served four years of a seven-year sentence for the second-degree murder of Gerald Adamant, a man who had inherited a fortune from his father at the age of fifty. At the time of his marriage to Helen Mackay, he was sixty-eight, she was twenty-four. The media soon dug up dirt on Helen, not that there was much. She had briefly appeared onstage at a risqué club, but apart from that, she's clean. Her family were found to be decent people with a daughter who, through no fault of her own, men lusted after. According to Helen, it was love for Adamant, the only person who had seen her inner self, and Adamant, if you remember, wasn't a bad-looking man. He certainly looked younger than his age, and she definitely looked older. The marriage cost plenty, the honeymoon even more, and for a few years, no more was heard of them, apart from Adamant's philanthropic work, his wife at his side.'

'And then?' Isaac said.

'Adamant is dead, Helen is charged with murder. According to her, the marriage was fine. He treated her well, she loved him. And then, one day, he snaps, accuses her of sleeping with other men, never loving him.'

'Any truth in his accusations?'

'No proof was ever found. The evidence at the trial showed that Gerald Adamant and his wife did have a good marriage, and there was no indiscretion by either person.'

'But she killed him.'

'The two of them are in the kitchen of their house. Renovations are going on, he's got his hands around her throat. She grabs hold of a hammer lying to one side and strikes him on the head to make him back off. Adamant died later that day. The rest you know.'

'Let us give the woman the benefit of the doubt,' Isaac said. 'Is there any information as to how she came to be working for Holden?'

'Holden was known for his frequent visits to the prisons throughout the country. On one of these prison visits, he befriends Helen Mackay – she's reverted to her maiden name – and subsequently makes an impassioned plea for her release, due to disputed evidence at her original trial.'

'Since her release, she's been vindicated of the crime,' Larry said.

'Carry on, Bridget.'

'Helen Mackay changed her name on her release. She had a degree in accountancy; his organisation needed an accountant. After a couple of years, Helen Langdon, as she is now known, was largely forgotten.'

'She was living well in Kensington,' Wendy said.

'Adamant's family, supporters of hers during the original trial, bequeathed her the apartment and sufficient money to live.'

'She wasn't entitled to more?'

'A pre-nuptial had been signed. Technically, she was entitled to nothing, but Adamant was a good man, so was his family, and Helen had made the man happy, even if she ultimately killed him.'

'It's one hell of a story,' Larry said.

'Life is often stranger than fiction,' Isaac said.

***

Violet Holden, as distraught as she was, realised the situation was delicate. Her husband, believed by the man in the street to be a moral man, had a dark side. Not that she had been under any illusion for many years, not since the first time he had erred. Back then, their son was up and walking, no more than one year old, and in walked the father, a look of guilt on his face.

That time he had confessed, as he would every time afterwards. That was why she had been able to tell the police in all honesty that her husband had only been with Helen the one time. If he had lived, he would have come back to the family home and confessed, and each time there'd be the pledge that he would never do it again. Violet knew full well that he would; not often, but often enough.

'Why was he with her?' Linda Holden, the younger child of James and Violet, said. Her mother knew that Linda was an unattractive woman of thirty-three, having inherited her father's bulbous nose and his blotchy skin, and her mother's slender

12

frame. The mother consoled herself with the knowledge that her daughter had a kind heart, like her father.

'It's not the first time,' her mother replied.

'But Helen, why her?'

Violet, an attractive woman, a beauty in her youth, knew why, even if the daughter did not. Helen Langdon, regardless of her history, was a beautiful woman, the sort of woman that her husband liked.

Violet remembered when they had met, she and James. He had not been a handsome man, but he had an inner strength, an inherent sense of decency. He was also the most intelligent man she had ever met, able to converse about any subject that interested her. They had become a couple, and they married within six months; he, a virgin, she, not so chaste.

They had been happy years before their son had come along, time enough for James to be elected to parliament. Even then he had been an ardent moralist, a clear and concise debater, a man going places, and in politics that meant the prime ministership. But then, another general election and James Holden was in opposition, a repeating event in the intervening years until his death. It was that first time he realised he had joined the wrong party, but there was no changing. He was not like Winston Churchill who had managed to move across the political divide; he was James Holden, a loyal party member, an ardent believer in doing the right thing, regardless of personal cost.

'She was devoted to your father, you knew that,' Violet Holden said.

'But why the two of them in bed?'

'There was empathy between the two of them, almost a melding of the minds. It's as if they were father and daughter.'

'How could he? It's almost obscene.'

'It was inevitable. Your father, like all great men, needed to rebel occasionally.'

'Are you saying that Helen offered herself as the object of his rebellion?'

'Helen would have done anything for him.'

'Aren't you upset, Mother?'

'Your father's legacy must be preserved; his good work must continue. Linda, you must be the one.'

'But I don't have my father's skills.'

'Yes, you do. It is for all of us to be willing to portray my husband, your father, as the man he was, a man who was flawed. His indiscretion with Helen must be used to portray him as a sinner who repents, a man who would admit all to his family.'

'And Helen?'

'She was a good person, regardless of her past and what has occurred. We will not conduct vendettas against anyone. We, the Holdens, will be the face of equanimity, of kindness, of charity to all.'

'It'll be hard for John,' Linda said.

'Then we must work hard to bring him around. He has a mean streak, and he will want to portray Helen as a wicked woman.'

'Not as someone he loved, but who ultimately rejected him for his father.'

'Precisely, and John doesn't have your and your father's kind nature,' Violet said.

Chapter 3

Isaac recognised trouble, not with a capital T, but with a capital C: Caddick. The man was sitting in Isaac's office; he appeared to be friendly, which meant only one thing, he was going to be difficult.

'Now, look here, Cook, I want this case run by the book. Commissioner Davies is taking a keen interest in this police station, especially this department, and James Holden was well respected. There's bound to be a lot of focus on us to provide results.'

'On me,' Isaac corrected the man.

'You think you're so smart, don't you? Well, let me tell you, I'm the superintendent, you're not, and unless your attitudes changes, I'll have you out of here in a flash.'

So much for the friendly, Isaac thought. He could see the hand of the commissioner in Caddick; he was not going to rise to the bait.

'We've just taken on the case. You're not expecting us to solve it that quickly, are you?' Isaac replied.

'I am. The demands on my budget are too much as it is. I'll not be paying for you and your mollycoddling of your people. And if your sergeant is too old, replace her. I can find you someone else, younger, keener, more willing to get out there and mix it on the street.'

'Sergeant Gladstone pulls her weight. She'll not let this department down.'

'On your head. I'm just giving you fair warning.'

Straight out of the Alwyn Davies book of policing, Isaac thought but decided to say no more. His superintendent had irritated him, not for the first time either. Isaac had wanted to tell the man that he was a snivelling little weasel, not even competent to shine the boots of his predecessor, Detective Chief Superintendent Goddard. Goddard had confided to Isaac that the forces were continuing to rally, and ongoing discussions were being conducted to allow Commissioner Davies to resign with grace, which would probably amount to a hefty payout, and possibly a knighthood.

Isaac had baulked at the mention of the knighthood. 'I thought they were awarded after you had done something, not destroyed it.'

'That's not how the real world works, and you know it,' Goddard had replied.

There was plenty to do, but Caddick's visit had left Isaac devoid of enthusiasm. He got up from his desk and walked out of his office.

Isaac sat down next to Wendy Gladstone. He could see she was struggling, and Caddick was right in that her performance was down from a year previously. He also knew that he would protect her at all costs. The times when she was needed out on the street, she had never let him down, and she was totally loyal to him, as were the others in the office. Isaac knew that Caddick's approach did not work. People under pressure perform as long as that pressure is reasoned and progressive, not by threatening their jobs.

'We need to find out why they were shot,' Isaac said. 'What do we know about Helen Langdon?'

'I can check out where she worked, talk to her colleagues. They're bound to be in shock after the executive director and the financial controller are both killed.'

'And in the same bed. Let's go, I'll come with you,' Isaac said. 'After five minutes with our senior, I need to be out of here.'

'Begging your pardon, sir, but Superintendent Caddick is a pain in the rear end,' Wendy said.

'Don't even think it, don't ever say it. You know how we're meant to act with the man.'

'It's hard. Sometimes I feel that I could tell him what I think of him.'

'I know what you mean,' Isaac said. 'Where's Larry?'

'He's back out at the crime scene. The CSIs are wrapping up. He wants to see what he can find out.'

'If it's a professional slaying, then probably not much.'

'There are still cameras in the street. Bridget can look through them once we have some idea of the murderer. She's collating what she can find on Holden and Langdon. It's a sorry mess, that's what it is.'

'A mess. I'm not so sure about the sorry. James Holden can only blame himself.'

'What did you make of Holden's wife?' Wendy asked.

'There's not much to say. She looked upset.'

'She was, but she wasn't surprised her husband had been in another woman's bed.'

'How can you know?'

'I observed her reactions when she spoke. She wasn't happy about the situation, although she was shocked it was Helen Langdon.'

***

The offices of James Holden's organisation were located in Paddington, no more than a six-minute drive from Challis Street. Isaac parked the car in a bay reserved for the executive director. 'He'll not need it today,' he said.

Inside the office, freshly painted judging by the smell, a middle-aged woman sat behind reception. 'Can I help you?' she said.

'Detective Chief Inspector Cook, Sergeant Gladstone,' Isaac said.

'You're here about James?'

'That's correct.' Isaac took note of the fact the woman did not mention Helen.

'It's a sad day. Everyone's a bit lost. His daughter's here if it's any help.'

'It will be.'

Isaac and Wendy took a seat. Isaac flicked through some brochures on the table in the reception area; Wendy checked the news on her phone. After a few minutes, Linda Holden appeared.

'We've been discussing what to do. We need to make a press statement.'

'I'll be asked to give a press conference at some stage,' Isaac said.

The three walked through the offices to the rear of reception. It was a better office than Homicide, Wendy had to admit.

'What can I do for you?' Holden's daughter said. 'As you can understand, I'm not really in the mood to answer too many questions. I should be with my mother.'

'That's understood. In fact, we're surprised to see you here.'

'I wouldn't be, but my father's work is important. It can't be allowed to fail.'

'Tell us, how do you plan to handle your father's death? How will you word your press statement?' Wendy said.

'How can we be accurate and ignore the fact he was murdered?'

'You can't,' Isaac said, 'but you're the second person in this office who has purposely not mentioned Helen Langdon.'

'We decided the best way to deal with the media would be for us not to mention Helen.'

'She worked here?' Isaac said.'

Yes, and very efficiently.'

'Then some advice. Don't ignore her, and don't try to hide the fact she was in bed with your father.'

'We thought it would be best.'

'Maybe you did, and if you were dealing with friends and relatives, then fine, but you're not. You're dealing with the British press, and they'll smell a rat if you try to hide the truth.'

'Then what do we say?'

'Words to the effect that tragically James Holden and Helen Langdon were killed in Bayswater today. The full details of how they died and what the motive was behind the slayings are still unclear. The police are conducting an investigation, and it would be inappropriate to comment further until more information is available. In the meantime, the good work of Mr Holden and his team of loyal supporters will continue.'

'You said everything without saying it,' Linda Holden said. 'You've not lied. You've acknowledged that Helen was killed, yet you've given no details.'

'And later on, when the press continues to pry?'

'The matter is with the police. It would be inappropriate to comment or speculate.'

'But everyone will know the truth.'

'It'll be headline news tomorrow, but you've not fuelled the fire.'

'Thank you. We'll follow your advice. I've made a note of what you just said.'

'Now, coming back to our investigation. What is your position in the organisation?'

'I was here in an advisory capacity, but now I'll be taking my father's position.'

'Are you qualified?' Wendy asked.

'I hope so. My father schooled me well in his beliefs. Beliefs I share as well.'

'Your father has died, upsetting in itself, no doubt. What we need to know is why?'

'My father did not make enemies intentionally, and he was not a firebrand. He was pragmatic, fully cognisant that in all of us is the need to rebel, to be bemused by the frailties of the human condition. He only wanted to control the descent into barbarism, not to curtail it totally.'

'Barbarism?'

'My father believed society was descending into a moral abyss as a result of modern technology. His opponents portrayed him as puritanical, against anything and everything. He was not that, but he held views, dated in modern society, which he put forward. He was vigorously opposed to the gratuitous sex and violence that pervade our lives.'

'There are people making fortunes out of those. They would be powerful enemies.'

'Potentially, but my father had little impact. However, I will continue the fight on his behalf and in his memory.'

'Helen Langdon?'

My father had in the last few years become passionate in his desire to modernise the penal system in this country, more in line with the Scandinavian countries, where a prisoner is treated with respect, where conjugal visits are allowed, and for the more trusted, weekend leave. He saw the current system in England as regressive, whereby the felon is punished, not redeemed.'

'Helen Langdon?'

'She is not the only one that my father helped. He met her three years ago in prison. He spent time with her, as he did with the other prisoners, but her case seemed unique. The press had lambasted her when she married Gerald Adamant, criticised her when she gave the impression of loving her husband when she had given them no cause to doubt her sincerity.'

'Did you like Helen?' Wendy asked.

'Yes, I did, so did everyone in this office. Not forsaking her beauty, and the fact that most men swooned in her presence, she was a capable and devoted member of the team.'

'Is that for us, or is that a genuine answer?'

'It's genuine. Even the Adamant family spoke for her at her retrial. It's unlikely they would have done so if they had any doubts.'

'At the first trial?' Isaac asked

'They still spoke on her behalf, but the public interest was too intense. An acquittal then would have received too much negative comment. Helen served her time and then came here.'

'Her relationship with your father?'

'She was devoted to him.'

'Intimate?'

'Not that any of us knew. Their relationship seemed to transcend the physical. What they have done has shocked us all.'

'Was your mother shocked?'

'Inspector Cook, my father was not a saint, nor was he a martyr. He was a man, the same as you. No doubt he had the same desires and lusts that we all do, yet he kept them in check most of the time.'

'It was not the first indiscretion?'

'It was to me, although my mother may say otherwise. Whatever the outcome of his and Helen's murders, I will hold my father in the highest esteem.'

'And Helen?'

'If she had erred, the same as my father, then we will forgive her.'

***

Larry questioned the concierge at the hotel in Bayswater, although the title of concierge pinned to the lapel of the man's collar seemed inappropriate. A third-rate hotel in Bayswater was not the Savoy, and the so-called deluxe suite where the two bodies had been discovered was neither luxurious nor well-maintained.

'I found them there, lying on the bed,' the concierge said. 'I saw them come in. I thought she was on the game, and he was one of her marks. How was I to know it was high and mighty James Holden.'

'You've heard of the man?'

'Who hasn't, always preaching to the converted. For me, I do what I want, when I want, and watch what I want. It's alright for him, rich and powerful. If he wants a woman, he can get one anytime.'

'And the woman he was with?'

'She oozed a good time. No doubt that's what he got until someone put a bullet through his head. Shame about her, though.'

'Why?'

'Good looker. Would have fancied her myself. Mind you, if she were selling herself, it would have taken more than a week's salary for a night with her.'

'She wasn't selling herself. She was a colleague.'

'He may have been an old fool, but I'll give him his due, he knew how to pick his colleagues. In this hotel, there are only the cleaners, the day manager, and a lady who does the accounts. I wouldn't give any of them one, but Holden's woman, anytime.'

Larry studied the man: overweight, the top button of his shirt undone. His hair was long and greased back. Altogether, a poor specimen of a hotel employee, and someone who wouldn't be averse to looking through a crack in a door to watch the action.

'Who did they sign in as?'

'Mr and Mrs Smith, what else?'

'Do they still do that? Larry asked.

'Of course not. Bob Cleveland and Mary Gold.'

'This is a murder, not the time for you to make cheap attempts at humour.'

'It's not the first body in this hotel. The occasional guest dies here; first murder, though. Will it be on the news tonight?'

'It probably will. If you're interviewed for the television, I should remind you that we'll be watching. If you attempt to gain financially or if you're withholding vital information, then you will be charged with perverting the course of justice, do you understand?'

'I understand, I've been through the rigmarole before.'

'You've been in prison?'

'Two years for stealing. This hotel is the only place that would give me a job.'

'If you want to keep it, what's the truth?'

'Okay, he's been here before.'

'With the woman?'

'No, another one.'

'Her name?'

'She's a regular around here. No one signed in. He just paid his money, the same as he always does, and I gave him the key. It's not recorded in the books.'

'Which means you've made yourself some money on the side.'

'A few of the local women use this place. It's not much, but it's discreet. No wonder Holden brought the classy woman here. Mind you, she looked better than this place. Who was she, by the way?'

'You'll find out soon enough. In the meantime, I need a statement and a proof of address from you. Any peepholes in the doors or the walls upstairs?'

'I'm not into that. I've done my time, been punished. That's the problem with all of you. Once a criminal, always a criminal.'

'They're both dead, upstairs in your hotel. Where were you? What did you hear?'

'Nothing. They were up on the third floor, and this is an old building, not like the type they build these days.'

'Are there any cameras in here?'

'Only in reception.'

'We'll need the video.'

'It hasn't worked for six months, and it's not me, it's the management. They don't want to waste the money.'

'Someone came into this hotel and killed two people. Did you see anyone suspicious?'

'There's always one or two that look suspicious, but they come in with a local whore.'

'These local women, where do they live, who are they? We'll need to interview them, as well as the men they were with.'

'Not much chance there, and they don't sign in, just slip me the money.'

'Your job after this becomes known?'

'Non-existent. Yet again, a man trying to reform is forced back into crime by those upholding it.'

'Work with me, and I'll make sure you keep your job. How do I contact your management?'

'To report me?'

'No. To let them know that I'll be giving you an assistant for a few nights and that you, as the concierge, have been more than helpful.'

Chapter 4

John Holden attempted to be busy, but he could not focus. Not only was there the distraction of his dead father, but there was also the increasing media interest in how he died, and how the man had been in bed with a woman younger than his daughter, a woman that the man's son had come to love.

Not that there had ever been any physical contact with Helen. As she had freely admitted when John had pledged his desire to be with her, it was the father she loved, not the son.

There was a client Holden needed to deal with, a man who would require all of John Holden's legal skills, yet he could not give the man what he wanted. He knew he should be upset over his father's death, but he could only feel sadness for Helen, as well as the hurt he had felt when she had been found in bed with his father. James Holden, he knew, was a fraud. He had seduced his son's one true love, even though John had confessed this love to him on more than one occasion.

Helen's reply to John had always been the same: 'My need of men has passed. They have only caused me problems.' John knew it was only the talk of someone who had spent four years in jail. Helen Langdon was a woman who needed a man, a woman who needed him, but she had rejected him, discarded him as if he was an old sock.

John Holden was angry, and his anger could not be abated. He wanted to sit down and cry, he wanted to lash out, he wanted someone to pay, but the person responsible was dead. He had never been fooled by his father, an eccentric who went around preaching goodness and love and family values, yet couldn't keep his trousers on if there was an attractive woman nearby. And it wasn't as if the man was handsome, not like the son. Holden got up from where he was sitting and stood in front of a mirror in his office in Mayfair. He studied his features.

'Perfection,' he said out loud. So loud that his personal assistant in the other room knocked on his door. 'Are you alright, Mr Holden?'

'Fine, thank you,' he replied. He straightened his tie, dabbed at the moistness around his eyes, and opened the door to the other room. 'I'll see my next client now,' he said.

***

Seth Caddick did not like DCI Isaac Cook, the senior investigating officer in Homicide at Challis Street. He needed to remove him from his position and to bring in his man, someone who would respect him, the same way he respected Commissioner Davies.

Caddick, a realist, knew that Isaac was competent, but he was not his police officer, he was the former superintendent's, the high and mighty Richard Goddard, a man who could play the political game as well as he could. A man who had succeeded because he had been friendly with the previous commissioner, Lord Shaw, and now Cook, Goddard, and Shaw were plotting to bring down Alwyn Davies. Caddick knew he had to do his part; he had to get rid of Cook.

'Watch out for Cook, the man's no fool,' Alwyn Davies had said in his office at Scotland Yard the previous day. 'Caddick, you're my man, and I'll protect you, but you're not up to the standard required for a superintendent.'

'I thought I was doing a good job,' Caddick had protested.

'You're not listening. You've succeeded well enough by claiming credit for others' work. No problem in itself, it happens all the time. Politicians claim they fixed the economy when the previous government had put in place the plans for recovery. I've claimed credit for the previous commissioner's efforts, and you've claimed credit from Goddard and Cook.'

'What are you saying?'

'The honeymoon period's over. It's up to you to prove yourself. It's for you to make your mark.'

'And how am I meant to do that?'

'You need Cook out and our man in. Cook's good on his feet, and with an audience that's listening, he's believable. You're good as well, but you don't look as impressive as Cook. People instinctively are drawn to him.'

'Is that an insult, sir?' Caddick asked. He was not used to criticism, especially from Davies.

'It's a fact, and you've got to do something about it.'

'I'm doing the best I can. We're bringing in the results.'

'You're not, Cook is. Is our man ready to take over from Cook?'

'He's available.'

'Then you need him, and soon. Goddard's in the background, stirring the pot.'

'Can't you transfer him out?'

'Goddard's got powerful friends. Men who are looking for the opportunity to pounce and evict me from this office. I've no intention of giving them the satisfaction, and you're not helping.'

'If you can't get rid of Goddard, then how can I get rid of Cook?'

'You've got to ride the man, you've got to prove he's not doing his job. His team, what about them?'

'They're loyal to him. I tried to get rid of Sergeant Gladstone. She's getting close to retirement, and she's not in the best of health.'

'And?'

'Cook said she was fine.'

'Is she?'

'She's Cook's person.'

'What have you done about it?'

'Nothing more at present.'

'Then do something. Get her checked out, make sure her health is up to scratch. What about her policing skills, reporting?'

'She's not computer literate.'

'Then subject her to the full treatment. Make sure she's on the list for early retirement, but whatever you do, you've got to undermine Cook, get him out. His replacement is a good man. He can do Cook's job, you can't.'

'But...'

'Don't but me, Seth. I'm under pressure, and if I go, you'll not be far behind. I put you in Goddard's position to support me, and so far, you've been a liability. At some stage, when they're ratcheting up the pressure on me, they'll be looking at my appointees and those I've sidelined, and you'll be subjected to a full audit of your policing skills, your ability to perform as a superintendent. And you know what they'll find?'

'No, sir.'

'They'll find someone who has been promoted without the necessary checks, and it'll reflect on me. I'm giving you two months with this, and then...'

'Goddard?'

'If it gives me a few months, I'll put him back at Challis Street.'

'But they'll see it as a weakness on your part.'

'What do I care, as long as I'm still in a job.'

'And me?' Caddick asked.

'Don't worry, I'll find you somewhere else.'

***

With Larry following up on the other woman who had been at the hotel in Bayswater with James Holden, Isaac and Wendy took the opportunity to make contact with the Adamant family.

Gerald Adamant, the dead patriarch, had inherited a mansion and its expansive grounds from his father on his death. His father had made a fortune in business; his son, Gerald, had every intention of enjoying the wealth.

He had been in his late twenties when he had married his first wife, the daughter of an investment adviser. Soon, in rapid succession, two children, Archie then Abigail.

'We're here because of the death of Helen, your father's third wife,' Isaac said. A maid brought in tea for those in the visitor's room of the Adamants' Victorian mansion. Also present were Archie, Abigail, now forty-one, and Howard, the son of Adamant's second wife. He was twenty-nine, and as Isaac had observed, not as impressive a figure as his step-siblings.

Archie was forty-three. He was erect, well-spoken. His sister, Abigail, was attractive. Not as beautiful on the eye as Helen Langdon had been, but still agreeable. Wendy thought she looked like someone who was into horses. The youngest, Howard, sat casually on a sofa. He was wearing a tee-shirt and jeans. Wendy's summation was that he spent the father's money, did little to earn any for himself.

'We had great respect and love for Helen,' Archie said. 'Her death has come as a shock to us.'

'She killed your father. How could you feel anything but loathing for the woman?'

'She made him happy.'

'And you loved your father that much, you agreed to him marrying a woman younger than any of you?'

'Not at first. We were suspicious of her motives, and her first impression in this house was not favourable. She was all over our father, and exceedingly pleasant to us.'

'Sickening,' Abigail said.

'And what about you, Howard?' Wendy asked.

'I didn't like it, especially when she tried to mother me.'

'Let me explain on behalf of Howard,' Archie said. 'Howard had found Helen on the internet. He's good with technology, that's why he makes more money than either my sister or myself.'

Wendy realised she had judged the cover, not the book, in the case of Howard Adamant.

'I write programs for computers. People buy them, I make a bundle,' Howard said, slightly more interested than before.

'She was more Howard's age,' Archie said. 'He didn't like it because he fancied her.'

28

'And what's wrong with that. She was a good-looking woman,' Howard said. 'You couldn't keep your eyes off her.'

'I'm not saying I could.'

'We are aware of Helen's attributes. We've been told about her by the Holden family.'

'How are they taking it?'

'Stoically. How about you three?'

'In time, Helen proved to us that she cared for our father,' Abigail said. 'To him, she was his wife, to us, she was a sister. We all grew very fond of her. Our mother, Archie's and mine, had died young, and then Howard's mother passed away a few years ago. Both wives had loved him, as he had them.'

'Is there any more that we should know about your mothers?' Isaac asked.

'Howard's mother was a few years younger than our father. Our mother was the same age as him,' Abigail said. 'Our father was a well-respected member of society, who we thought at first had gone slightly mad when he arrived at the house with Helen.'

'Trying to regain lost youth with a younger woman,' Archie said.

'Much younger,' Howard said, 'and yes, I did fancy Helen. I wanted her, even made a pass at her, but she wasn't like that. She looked it, but she was a decent person.'

'Your relationship with her, eventually?'

'I still fancied her, and she knew it. It became a joke between us, nothing more. I'll not say a bad word about her.'

'Yet the woman killed your father?' Isaac said.

'Helen had seen a change in his behaviour for a few months. She had confided in us, asked our advice,' Abigail said.

'And what did you say?'

'We pleaded with our father to see a specialist, but he wouldn't hear of it. Our father was conscious of his own mortality, and he wasn't willing to admit he was getting old.'

'The young wife?'

'At first, but he loved Helen as much as she loved him.'

'And your reaction when your father died?' Wendy asked.

'We were shocked and upset. We blamed Helen, called her some wicked things, but then came the autopsy, and the pathologist stating our father had a brain tumour and it could have been responsible for his aggression. They did find bruising around Helen's neck.'

'Did you speak to Helen before her trial?'

'I did,' Abigail said. 'She was contrite, emotional, and sorry for what she had done.'

'Did you believe her?'

'I wasn't sure what to believe. She had killed our father, the result of a violent confrontation. At the trial, the first trial, the experts for the defence and the prosecution were arguing as to whether a brain tumour could have been responsible for our father's aggression.'

'And what did you believe?'

'We all wanted to believe that Helen was innocent. She was family, she was important to us.'

'At the first trial, you, Archie, made a plea on behalf of the family.'

'It was obvious Helen was going to prison, but the experts were in conflict. We just wanted it to be known we did not hold any blame against her.'

'It's an unusual reaction,' Isaac said. 'Normally, the family of the deceased are vehement in their condemnation. Why are you so different?'

'Because we knew our father, we knew Helen. If it had been us, we would have acted in the same way.'

'Had it happened before?'

'Once or twice. He hit me once for no reason,' Abigail said.

'And when was this?'

'When I broached the idea of him visiting a specialist.'

'Was anyone else present?'

'It was only me.'

'Had Helen raised the subject with him?'

'On one occasion. He didn't like it, but he didn't hit her. She was afraid to talk to him again, that's why I tried.'

'Your stepmother was in jail. What did you do?'

'Archie's a lawyer. He put together a team to examine the evidence. That's when we came across James Holden.'

'You knew the man?'

'We all did. He visited Helen in jail. I went with him the first time,' Abigail said.

'After that?'

'He'd go on his own, once or twice a month. We could see whenever we visited her that she was becoming enamoured of Holden, not that we discouraged it.'

'It was Holden who managed to get her out of prison,' Isaac said.

'He approached us, asked us to write a letter stating our non-objection, and in time she was released. Six months after her release, new evidence from another expert showed that more research had been done in America on the effect of a brain tumour pressing on certain parts of the brain. It was accepted, and the conviction against Helen was quashed.'

'Did you keep in contact after her release?'

'We did, not often though. Helen seemed to want the past behind her, and we understood. She was always welcome here though, and she'd phone occasionally. I doubt if we saw her more than three or four times since her release.'

'And now, to find out that she has been in bed with Holden?' Isaac said.

'We knew of her affection for the man, but he was married,' Abigail said. 'We reserve our judgement on Helen, but we'll never waiver in our support for her. She was an important part of our father's life.'

Outside the mansion, as Isaac and Wendy were preparing to leave, he asked 'What did you make of what they said?'

'Helen Langdon is either due for sainthood, or we've been fed nonsense.'

'They did support her at the trials. For Helen's benefit, or was there an ulterior motive?'

'You don't buy their holier than thou attitude?' Wendy said.

'Too good to be true,' Isaac said. 'Get Bridget to dig in the dirt, find out what she can about the Adamants.'

Chapter 5

With Helen Langdon, née Mackay, identified as the woman who had been killed with James Holden, as well as the woman who had killed Gerald Adamant, public sentiment towards her vacillated. Some saw her as the callous murderer of an old husband; others, as the falsely maligned and loyal wife of a man who had gone mad. Her parents' home was surrounded by the press and gawping onlookers when Isaac and Wendy arrived. Barricades had been erected in the street, a uniform stationed at the front door.

'It's been madness,' the uniform said. 'The poor parents inside are doing their best to cope, and the mongrels outside are making it into a party. We even had an ice-cream van parked on the other side of the road. It was doing sterling business until we moved it on.'

Isaac had seen it too many times. A murder, someone's misfortune, and the bizarre, the plain nosey, were incapable of showing any compassion for those trying to deal with the emotions and the raw nerves. Mr and Mrs Mackay seemed to be two such people.

'Helen, she was a good daughter,' her father said.

'I'm sorry,' Isaac said, 'but I must ask you certain questions.'

'We understand,' her softly spoken mother said. 'We've not slept since it happened, not certain if we will ever again.'

Wendy could see the emotions on their faces. She felt as if she should go over and put her arm around the mother but decided not to. It was a formal interview, and the parents may have some information that would not be revealed if there was overfamiliarity.

'When did you last see your daughter?' Isaac asked.

'The day she died. She popped in for a cup of tea, unannounced.'

'Her mood?'

'She was cheerful, enjoying being unknown.'

'She would be known around here?' Wendy said.

'Not here. We moved from our previous house. The notoriety was too much, the parents of a murderer, not that we ever believed it.'

'Why? Your daughter married an older man. If I'm not mistaken, Gerald Adamant was older than you, Mr Holden.'

'He was. He wanted to call me Dad. I wasn't having any of it. It was always Gerald and Frank whenever we met.'

'Was that often?'

'Not often. Helen, she was busy with Gerald's philanthropic pursuits, but she phoned every week. Once we had got over the initial shock of the age difference, we accepted them as a married couple.'

'Did Helen have a penchant for older men?'

'Do you mean, was she wiggling her arse to seduce them? Is that what you're saying?'

'Frank, she's our daughter. You can't say that about her,' Betty, Helen's mother, said.

'It's what they said in the newspapers. It's what the two police officers here want to ask, but they'll be polite. Am I correct, Inspector Cook?'

'I would have used different wording, but yes.'

'You know of Helen's history. It was the same when she was young. Fourteen and then she starts filling out. The local youths can't handle it, but Helen's not like that. She was studious, always got good marks at school, and then she goes to university, a good degree, but what happens? The boss is after her, the men in the office fancy their chances, but all Helen wants is to do her job, meet a nice man, and settle down. She tried it once, lived with him for a few months, the date is set for the marriage, and then he takes off. After that, she's upset, so she appears onstage at a club.'

'We're aware of this?'

'Bare breasts, plenty of flesh. Not that Helen liked it, but she had become tired of using her brain, only for men to see below her neck. Anyway, after a year or so, Gerald walks into her life. We warned her about older men, but she said she was fine with him, and she was. At least, up until that fateful day when he tried to kill her, and she hit him with the hammer.'

Wendy could see the mother sobbing. She relented and went and put her arm around the distraught woman; Isaac understood why she did so. He had once had to tell the parents of a young man of seventeen that he had blown himself up and twenty others in a terrorist attack. The memory of the mother's reaction still haunted him, even after so many years.

'Your relationship with the Adamants?'

'The younger son could be surly, but he was decent enough, the same as his brother and sister.'

'Surly?'

'He fancied Helen, more her age than his father was, but she was committed to Gerald, and the younger son, a smart man by all accounts, wasn't her kind of man. She told us he reminded her of all the men she had met before. She offered them companionship and an intelligent woman. All they saw was a quick lay. Apologies for my speaking about my daughter like that, but with us, Helen was very open. It was the way we liked it with her. She wasn't only our daughter, she was also our friend.'

'The Adamants supported her at her trial.'

'They did, and very commendable of them, but with so much publicity, and Helen looking the way she did, the sentiment of the jury was against her. We used to visit her in prison at every opportunity, and then, there was James Holden.'

'Did you meet him?'

'On many occasions. Another decent man, the same as Gerald.'

'Older?'

'Helen had enjoyed being married to Gerald. He treated her well, never flaunted her, and he always included her in his conversations, entrusted her to help with his philanthropic work.

35

She told us that James Holden was the same as Gerald and he was going to get her out of prison. We could see she was becoming close to the man, and even though he was married, and we warned her, the heart doesn't know such boundaries.'

'After her release?'

'She went to work for Holden, although the salary wasn't much. Not that Helen needed it. The Adamants ensured she had an apartment and some money.'

'I must ask this,' Isaac said. 'Helen, as you say, was a good person, so was Holden, yet they ended up in a hotel together.'

'We've tried to understand why,' Betty Mackay said, temporarily revived by Wendy's ministrations. 'As much as she may have loved James, he was still married. She would not have considered it for one moment, not our Helen.'

'But she did. The facts are clear, and we need to know why. Mr Mackay, do you have any thoughts?'

'No more than my wife. Helen would have only agreed if it was for James's well-being, but he was older than me. The passion doesn't run as strong, the need to rush off to a hotel for a little romance doesn't seem plausible. That's more the folly of teenagers in love, not an old man and one of his employees.'

'Regardless, it did happen,' Isaac said, 'and not only that, we know that James Holden had been there with another woman in the past.'

'Then we are lost as to why Helen was there with him unless it was important. Are you sure they were involved?'

'We're sure. There's proof.'

***

Two men waited in the reception of the hotel in Bayswater. Neither man was comfortable with the other: the concierge because his money-making venture, his time with one of the whores instead of payment, would be curtailed, and the other man, Police Constable Trevor Greenock, because he was fastidious about personal hygiene, and the concierge stank.

'What time does this woman come in?' Greenock asked.

'It depends. Some nights she doesn't come in at all.'

'Attractive?'

'I'd say so,' the concierge said, although not as attractive as the murdered woman had been, he knew that. He had seen them through the peephole, seen the old man's attempt at lovemaking, imagined it was him, young and virile, with her. If it had not been for the bell on reception, another whore bringing her mark in, he would have stayed watching Holden and the woman; he would have seen who shot them.

'It's not much of a hotel is it,' Greenock said. He was a tall man with black wavy hair. Two years with the police, and his first stakeout. He had changed his police uniform for an assistant manager's at the hotel. Tomorrow he'd have a talk to Homicide and see if he could move over on a more permanent basis.

'Some of the women who come in here aren't much either.'

'Then why was Holden here?'

'You'd better ask him.'

'He's dead, that's why I'm asking you,' Greenock said. He could sense the unpleasant man knew more than he was letting on.

'Sometimes men like a bit of the rough, a woman off the street. Men like Holden, I see them in here occasionally. They spend their lives being respectable, law-abiding citizens, when all they want to do is rebel, the same as all of us. But it's not possible, you know that, not in the long term anyway. They come down here. One was even a vicar, not that he realised that I knew.'

'How did you know?'

'My father, he was keen on the church. Every weekend we'd be there. Everyone gives away what and who they are by the way they walk, their mannerisms.'

'Regular Sherlock Holmes, aren't you?'

'Not me. I've read all his books, and he's right. You watch the next one that comes in.'

Soon after, a woman, dressed in a white blouse with a red skirt, walked in through the door. The man was dressed casually, an open-necked shirt, a pair of jeans.

'The usual, Joyce?' the concierge said.

'I'd say by the way he walked he was a police officer,' Greenock said.

'I'd have him down as an army officer. Why the police?'

'I've seen him around, not that I've ever spoken to him, and he didn't recognise me.'

'Any problem for him?'

'Not if he's off duty.'

A forty-five minute wait, another woman. 'It's her,' the concierge said.

'Excuse me. I'm Police Constable Greenock. I've a few questions if you don't mind.'

The man she had come in with attempted to rush out of the hotel. Greenock had pre-empted him by remotely locking the entrance door. 'You'll not get out of here. And besides, it's the lady that interests the police, not you.'

'I've not done anything,' the woman protested. 'I'm registered, legal, even pay my taxes.'

'I'm here about a man you brought in here in the past.'

'I'm like a priest. I don't tell on anyone. They pay their money, they have their fun, and that's it.'

'Your name, sir?' Greenock said, turning to the flustered man.

'It'll ruin me.'

'Were you here on the night of the murder?'

'I read about it, James Holden. This is my first time here.'

Greenock looked over at the concierge. He shook his head, indicating the man had lied.

'Okay, I'll tell you what we'll do. If you provide me with evidence as to who you are, you can leave now. I've got your photo, and I'll check your phone before you leave. I'll just take a few contacts off it, phone them up if we can't contact you, tell them that we're looking for a man who had been with a prostitute in Bayswater. I'm sure we'll find you soon enough.'

'Conrad Evans, I'm a builder in the city. I was on my way home. It's been a long day, and I see Daisy here, and she beckons me over. That's the truth, believe me.'

'I do. Your identification and your phone.'

Greenock picked up his phone while the man fumbled in his wallet. 'Send a car,' he said. 'You'll need to come to the station with me,' he said to the woman.

'What for? Business has been quiet. You'll have to feed me if you want to talk.'

'Pizza?'

'That'll do.'

Her client left, a police car arrived. 'I'll look past your taking backhanders from the whores this time,' Greenock said to the concierge.

'Don't worry. Your Inspector Hill fixed it with the management. I work with you; he'll protect me.'

'The long arm of the law protecting the villains. Whatever next?'

'It was the long arm of the law that put me inside in the first place.'

'You'll be here tomorrow?'

'I hope so. It's a lousy job, but it does have benefits.'

'Joyce?'

'You've got it.'

'You're a foul man,' Greenock said. 'Don't think tonight has been a pleasure for me.'

'I've got a thick skin. Nothing you say will affect me.'

'No doubt it won't. I hope you enjoy your time with Joyce.'

'More than you will with Daisy.'

Chapter 6

At Challis Street Police Station, the prostitute sat quietly in one corner, eating a pizza. 'Not much to look at,' Wendy said.

Isaac thought his sergeant was harsh in her criticism. He could see the woman had the look of the street and the needle marks on her arms were not the best, but considering the life the woman had led, she had fared better than most.

'What are you looking at?' the woman said, lifting her head away from the pizza.

'Nothing,' Isaac said. 'When you're ready.'

'Are you going to charge me?'

'There's no charge. We've just got a few questions.'

'Okay, let's get on with it. I've lost enough money tonight because of you.'

Inside the interview room, Daisy sat on one side, Isaac and Wendy on the other. 'Could we have your correct name, please?' Isaac said.

'Elizabeth Wetherington.'

'Miss Wetherington...'

'Call me Daisy, everyone else does.'

'Daisy, we are interested in a man you took to the hotel several times in the past.'

'How do you expect me to remember. I go there, they have what they want, and then they leave. I don't get to study them, not even talk to them most of the time.'

'According to the concierge, you took this man to the hotel two weeks ago on a Thursday. Can you remember back to that day?'

'My memory's not so good.'

'What does it need to help it?'

'Money would help.'

Wendy studied the woman: peroxide blonde, heavy on the make-up, bright-red lipstick, a drawn face.

'There's no money in here,' Isaac said. 'The best you could do is to give us your information and then you're out of here.'

'Okay, a Thursday two weeks ago. It was a busy night, made some good money.'

'And what's good money?' Wendy asked.

'Five hundred pounds at least.'

'And then you spent it shooting up.'

'Maybe I did, maybe I didn't.'

'I'll show you a photo,' Isaac said. 'If you recognise him, let me know.' Isaac pushed the photo of James Holden across the desk. Daisy picked it up and studied it for a few seconds.

'He always treated me well, paid more than the others.'

'Why did he pay more?'

'I don't know, guilt maybe. Some of them regret what they've done afterwards. Some of them are in tears because they've cheated on their wives.'

'Does that worry you?'

'The tears or the cheating?'

'The cheating.'

'Why? Should it? I'm not their social worker. I'm a working woman trying to survive. If they want me, they pay. If they don't, they can keep on walking by, but him, he doesn't. He phones me up, we meet outside the hotel, sometimes inside. We go up to the room, and that's it. Fifteen minutes later I'm back on the street looking for another man.'

'Not much of a life, is it?' Wendy said.

'I was married once. He used to beat me. Out on the street is better than that, and anyway, I'm used to it.'

'What can you tell us about the man in the picture?' Isaac said.

'He never gave me a name. He's polite, a little on the old side, but he manages.'

'With your help,' Wendy said.

'That's what he pays for. Once it's over, he gives me my money and leaves. He's not much into conversation. It's purely business. I've got the commodity, he's got the money.'

'Are there many like him?'

'Not many. Most of them are rough, drunk from a night out at the pub, some are violent.'

'Coming back to the man in question,' Isaac said. 'What else can you tell us about him.'

'Nothing really. As I said, he didn't talk much.'

'Why do you think he paid you for sex?'

'I've no idea. Most of them have an unhappy home life. Some want to tell me about it, but I'm not interested. But with him, nothing. I just assumed he wanted a bit of the rough.'

'And you're the rough?'

'You know what I mean. There's no baggage with me, no pretending it's love. It's into the room, strip down, a couple of minutes fumbling around, him on top of me, me on top of him, and that's it.'

'Clinical,' Wendy said.

'No doubt, but, as I said, I was married once. I don't want to pretend to be in love only to be thrown across the room on another night.'

'Do you watch the television, read the newspapers?' Isaac said.

'Not me. I've no time for television, and I'm not interested in the news.'

'The man we are questioning you about was murdered. Did you know that?'

'Not me.'

'He was murdered in the hotel where you met Constable Greenock. It was the room you normally use.'

'And you think I'm involved?'

'He was with another woman.'

'And I could have been murdered if I had been with him?'

'We don't think so. I suggest you read the newspaper in future. The man's name was James Holden. Have you heard of him?'

'Not me.'

'He's well known. A member of parliament, a moral campaigner.'

'And he was with me. If I'd known, I would have charged him double.'

'The woman's name was Helen Mackay. Have you heard of her?'

'Helen, sent to prison for murdering that old man?'

'Yes, that's her.'

'Before she latched on to him, we used to work together in Soho.'

'On the street?'

'Not Helen. She was down on her luck, the same as me, and we're in this club, strutting around with next to nothing on.'

'Was it a strip club?' Wendy asked.

'They called it a gentlemen's club, not that many of the customers were. All they wanted to do was to grab us, make us sit on their laps, and let them fondle our breasts.'

'And you let them?'

'Why not? They were generous with their tips.'

'And Helen, was she into this?'

'The men wanted her, more than me, more than any of the other girls.'

'You've not answered my question.'

'Helen kept her distance. She was a classy woman, and then, one day, she's gone. We were all envious of her, but she never fitted in.'

'Why's that?'

'As I said, she didn't belong. She was a beautiful woman, not like us.'

'You still look okay,' Wendy said.

'Sure, but Helen was in a league of her own. She could have made plenty of money, set herself up as a high-class escort.

She always said she wanted to settle down, find a man who treated her well. She was intelligent, advising us on how to live our lives, where to invest our money.'

'Were you and the other women resentful?'

'Of Helen? No way. We all loved her.'

'When she killed her husband?'

'I wanted to be a character witness, but her lawyer wasn't too keen. Anyway, in the end, her dead husband's family said a few words for her.'

'Were you at the trial?'

'Every day. I couldn't help her, but she was my friend.'

'When she came out of prison, did you make contact with her?'

'I contacted her once, but she was distant. It was clear she wanted to put the past behind her, so I left her alone.'

'And she ended up with your man in your room at the hotel.'

'I don't get that,' Daisy said.

'Nor do we. You're free to go,' Isaac said.

'I hope you find who did it. Helen was my friend. I'll be sad tonight. I think I'll go home.'

'What did you reckon?' Wendy said after Daisy had left, a police car organised to drop her one street from the flat she shared with another working girl.

'Holden wanted Helen, fixated on her, and he couldn't have her, but he can have an old friend.'

'There's more than a few psychoses there.'

'How did Holden know that Daisy wouldn't be at the hotel on the night he went with Helen? Why that hotel?'

'As I said, the man had some issues.'

'You're right,' Isaac said. 'We need to find out what they were.'

***

Isaac met up with Richard Goddard, Homicide's former chief superintendent. Caddick would have regarded it as gross disloyalty; Isaac considered it necessary.

'How is it in Public Relations?' Isaac asked as the two men sat down for lunch at a pub on the other side of the River Thames.

'It's a hard battle convincing anyone the Met is on top of their game. Commissioner Davies is making a right hash of it, and now he's planning to bring in another lackey to lord it over us.'

'Can he?'

'They're trying to get him out, but it takes time, and in the interim, he'll do what he wants.'

'Can't they stop him? There are procedures in place to control who is hired, who is fired.'

'The man's fighting back, pushing the envelope. He'll claim discretionary powers, and what is anyone going to do? Subject him to a disciplinary hearing, invite the press in to watch? Our commissioner is a caged animal. He'll do whatever's necessary to survive.'

'If you were in his position?'

'Are you saying I'm as bad as him?'

'Not at all, sir, but you're a political animal. Can't you play the system? Take some shortcuts, put Davies under pressure?'

'From Public Relations? It's hardly likely, and besides, I'm a chief superintendent. There's more than a few ranks separating me from Davies.'

'Then bring them on board.'

'Some are on board, but no one's willing to show their hand just yet.'

'And in the meantime, the Met goes down the tube, us with it?'

'Regardless of Davies and Caddick, you've got a job to do. What's the situation with James Holden?'

'Any murmurings from where you are?'

'There's concern at Westminster. The man was a politician, and they're all watching.'

'There'd be a few skeletons down there.'

'I know of some,' Goddard said.

'If Holden is held up to ridicule, then eventually the press will start looking into the behaviour of others.'

'They're always trying, but so far they've not found anything.'

'Why's that?'

'The relationship between those in power and those in influence is still strong.'

'Influence? You mean those who control the television channels and the newspapers?'

'Yes. Mind you, social media is an issue. That can't be controlled.'

'Holden wanted it curtailed,' Isaac said.

'He wanted to control the sex and the violence, not the truth.'

'That's the problem. Once you start putting clamps in place, you escalate into other areas that should be sacrosanct.'

'Freedom of the press?'

'Exactly.'

'Do you think the media moguls would care if Facebook and Twitter were throttled?'

'No. Is that what Holden was doing?'

'Indirectly.'

The two men had been talking for over thirty minutes and had not ordered. Isaac called over the waiter. 'Two of your specials, a bottle of wine.'

'What's the occasion?' Goddard said.

'It's good to be here, sir.'

'Caddick, how's he performing?'

'He's learning. He's picked up the clichéd responses, found himself some sycophants, as well as a lady to deal with his paperwork. She's efficient and apparently loyal.'

'Talk to her, find out if she is.'

'Undermine him from within?'

'Don't try it. That'll get you suspended. Those who are pandering to him, important?'

'No. They're moderate performers, but they'll keep him informed.'

'Then do your job, solve the case,' Goddard said. 'What is it with Holden? How come he gets himself murdered with a woman who had spent time in prison?'

'She was declared innocent at a retrial.'

'Maybe she was, but mud sticks, and it's stuck to Holden's legacy, threatening to undo his good work.'

'Good work?'

'His work with the prison system, that's well-founded. It was a creaking institution, in need of a clean broom. If his party had been elected to power, he would have become the Secretary of State for Justice. No possibility his death is politically motivated?'

'None we can see at the present moment.'

'Caddick is aiming to bring his man in to take your place,' Goddard said.

'He tried it once before.'

'This time he might succeed. Don't give Caddick a chance to unseat you.'

'Can I stop him?'

'Only by good policing.'

Chapter 7

Linda Holden, the head of the organisation that her father had set up to combat declining moral standards, realised she had been given the poisoned chalice. With her father's death, and his subsequent exposure as a man who preached one thing, did another, his star had fallen.

Isaac and Larry knew when they visited James Holden's offices that the man once held in such high esteem had erred more than once. According to Daisy, the prostitute, she had been four times in that hotel with him: the same room, the same bed.

Holden taking Helen Langdon there too, and using the same bed, seemed unusual.

Bridget was delving into the man's childhood, attempting to understand what drove him and whether it was hereditary. John Holden, the son, it had been found, had a history of violence when he was younger, a need to cause trouble. Isaac saw him as a possible suspect, but he would have had to know of his father's peccadilloes, as well as where he went with Helen and when.

'It's not been easy,' Linda Holden said. Isaac and Larry were in her office. Another lady had brought them a coffee each from the machine in the office kitchen. To Isaac, it was not up to the standard of the coffee he usually purchased at a café near Challis Street. However, he thanked the lady for her kindness.

'What do you mean?' Isaac said, looking at Linda. He could see she was struggling to manage, her desk cluttered with papers.

'My father was regarded by some as a saviour. A man who stood up for the common man, the decent man, but now...'

'Social pariah?'

'No one's listening. That's the problem: put yourself on a pedestal, and you're soon knocked off.'

'It was your father's doing,' Isaac said.

'And Helen's. We trusted her, even welcomed her into our home, and then she goes and sleeps with our father. Do you know why?'

'What did you know of Helen's past life?'

'I read the transcript of her first trial.'

'Then you know about the club.'

'Our parents taught us not to be judgemental, to take people as you find them.'

'With Helen, was that possible?'

'Yes. My opinion of her has been shaken, but I still regard her as a friend.'

'Then you must have some ideas as to why she was in that hotel with your father.'

'Was it the first time?'

'In that hotel with Helen, but he had been there before.'

'Who with?'

'A woman who had known Helen before she went to prison; before she married Gerald Adamant.'

'After my father met Helen, he had her checked out. She was in prison for killing her husband. My father had to be sure she was worthy of his help.'

'And what did he find out?'

'The report's here. I read it two days ago for the first time.'

'Damning?'

'I've made you a copy.'

'We'll read it back at Challis Street. Tell us, what did you gain from the report?'

Linda Holden sat back, reflected on what to say. 'Everyone she came into contact with had only good things to say about her. She had been an accountant before, competent according to her boss.'

'She had trouble with him.'

'She had that effect on men, even my brother.'

'What about him?'

'He was in love with her, but she rejected him.'

'How did he take it?'

'Badly.'

'Your brother, he doesn't seem as agreeable as you.'

'John got a temper, and he was upset over Helen. He blows hot and cold sometimes, but he was always polite with her, distant with my father.'

'No love lost?'

'My brother respected our father, although he didn't always follow his advice. There were a few instances when John was younger, drunkenness, occasionally sneaking a girl into his bedroom.'

'Normal for a young man,' Isaac said.

'Normal for me,' Larry said.

'My father wasn't upset over what he had done. My father was a pragmatist, but he had a reputation to uphold, a reputation that depended on his family, as well.'

'And a teen has hormones driving him in another direction.'

'Would your brother be capable of murder?' Isaac said.

'Not John. Don't think because I told you about him and my father that he'd be capable of that. He admired my father, loved Helen. He'd not do anything to either of them.'

'How about the people in this office? Some must have been suspicious of the special relationship between Helen and your father.'

'We all knew, even our mother, but we trusted Helen.'

Isaac was always suspicious when everyone told him that the person was a saint, would never harm a fly. Experience had taught him that everyone was flawed, even the righteous.

'What about you?' Isaac said. 'What's your secret?'

'What do you mean?'

'No one's perfect. Your father's been murdered. Nobody has the luxury of privacy. We'll dig deep if you don't tell us.'

'Apart from an inappropriate love affair in my twenties, there's nothing. I'm married now, have been for twelve years, two children.'

50

'Inappropriate?'

'He was married. It ended badly.'

'How?'

'His wife found out. There was a scene where she confronted us in the hotel room.'

'How did she find out?'

'I never knew. I was heartbroken, but time heals.'

'And the man?'

'He went back to her. I see them from time to time.'

'Socially?'

'Not socially, but we move in the same circles.'

'Anything said?'

'Nothing.'

'Does your husband know?'

'No.'

'Your father, your mother?'

'I can't be sure. And besides, it was a long time ago.'

***

James Holden's body was released from Pathology and handed over to the family. They had asked for respect and to be able to grieve in peace – it was not to happen.

At the church James and Violet Holden attended every Sunday, the vultures were waiting, cameras at the ready. Isaac had seen them on his arrival and had asked the uniforms to make sure they didn't get too close.

John and Violet Holden were the first to arrive. Soon after, Linda Holden, accompanied by her husband and two children. Isaac noticed a few politicians, everyone from James Holden's office.

'Not much of a showing,' Wendy said. She sat at the back of the church with Isaac. They hadn't been invited, but it was an excellent chance to watch the reactions of the people, to see if there were any unknown faces.

'Under the circumstances, it's the most that could be expected. The family's been ostracised since his murder. Why was he in that hotel?'

'With that woman.'

'It'll become clearer in time, but if Helen Langdon is so important, then why a flea-bitten hotel frequented by prostitutes?'

'You don't buy the idea that he may have had some sordid perversion, a need to demean Helen, to blame her for his weaknesses.'

'Not with her, I don't.'

'Then what?'

'I don't know. What do you reckon to the family?'

'His wife seems upset, so does his daughter. The son appears ambivalent.'

At the front of the church, the priest went through the funeral service, both John and Linda reading from the bible, Linda also delivering a eulogy, failing to mention the circumstances of her father's death.

At the end, the coffin was borne away on the shoulders of six men, one of them John Holden, another Linda's husband.

'What do we know about the husband?' Wendy said, as the coffin passed by.

'Married to Linda for twelve years, the CEO of a manufacturing company. Not much to tell about him.'

'Any reason to believe he might be involved?'

'You can check him out if you like, but I'm suspicious of John Holden. His alibi is weak for the night of the murder.'

'At home reading. A single man in his forties. It doesn't sound natural.'

'Gay?'

'He was keen on Helen.'

'Why Helen? He's not a bad-looking man. There must be plenty of opportunities for him.'

Outside the church, the cortege left, the hearse in front, two limousines carrying the Holden family following.

'Not much more to be gained here,' Wendy said.

'Caddick's trying to get me out. I've received some information.'

'What will you do?'

'Solve this case. He'll not act if I do, and he'll not act to remove me at this time.'

'He'll wait until the right time, take credit for your good work.'

'That's how it works,' Isaac said.

'Not in my book, it doesn't.'

'Your book's an old edition.'

'It's the edition I prefer.'

'This time, I intend to fight fire with fire.'

'You're going to take him on, get him out of Challis Street, bring back Chief Superintendent Goddard?'

'When the time's right.'

'That's not like you, guv.'

'These are unusual times. The old rules no longer apply.'

'Be careful. It could backfire.'

'That's why I'm forewarning you. I don't want anyone else involved.'

'We'll be right behind you, you know that.'

'I know, but I'll not be able to help you if I don't succeed.'

***

Back at Challis Street, Bridget Halloran was keen to bring the team together. 'I've been through the report that Linda Holden gave us,' she said.

The four were sitting in Isaac's office. 'What have you found?' Larry asked.

'I cross-referenced the club where Helen and Daisy had worked.'

'Anything interesting?'

'Ben Aberman, the owner of the club, disappeared while they were both working there.'

'Suspicious?'

'Not at the time. The man had incurred significant debt, and it was thought he had left the country. No one's ever reported him missing or attempted to find him.'

'Was the club a front for prostitution?' Wendy said.

'They all are,' Isaac said.

'According to what we know, Helen Langdon was not prostituting herself, although Daisy probably was.'

'Is there any more to Aberman disappearing?'

'The ownership of the club changed overnight.'

'And the debts?'

'They disappeared.'

'Are you suggesting Aberman was murdered?'

'It's a possibility. Also, his house has remained empty.'

'Men such as Aberman change their names all the time,' Larry said.

'That's why there's never been an investigation, and would the police be interested in the disappearance of a man such as Aberman?'

'Not unless there was a crime to answer for,' Isaac said.

'Is the club still operating?' Larry asked.

'I'll give you the address. Don't expect too much when you get there. It looks seedy.'

'We won't.'

'And don't touch the women,' Wendy said.

'Would we ever?' Larry replied.

***

Two funerals in as many days. The funeral of James Holden had been poorly attended; the funeral of Helen Langdon, née Mackay, not so. This time, the church was overflowing. In the front pew, Frank and Betty Mackay. Behind them Linda Holden and the three Adamants, Archie, Abigail, and Howard.

'We had to come,' Abigail Adamant said. 'A mark of respect for her.'

'The other people here?' Isaac said.

'They're supporters of what my father was trying to achieve, people that he's helped,' Linda Holden said, turning around from where she was sitting.

'They weren't present at your father's funeral.'

'Some were, but the others, they're fresh out of prison. They don't want publicity, and there were cameras at my father's.'

'There are cameras outside.'

'Most of them came in through a side entrance. I organised a bus for them, and besides, Helen was one of them.'

Abigail Adamant read from the bible, one of the women who had come on the bus gave a eulogy about what an inspiration Helen had been. Linda Holden also got up and made a speech on behalf of Helen, noting that she was an exceptional woman and their lives had been better for knowing her. No mention was made of James Holden.

At the end of the service, Helen's father, Archie and Howard Adamant, as well as three men from the bus, carried the coffin to the waiting hearse. Isaac gave Wendy his handkerchief as she was overcome with emotion. 'It's so sad,' she said.

'What was she, do we know?' Isaac said.

'Not really, although I feel sad for her parents.'

'We've got work to do. I need to go with Larry to this club.'

Chapter 8

The night of Helen Langdon's funeral, two men entered the Dixey Club in Bayswater. 'It's not much,' Larry said. Both men were dressed casually, no ties, no signs of being police officers.

'Do you want to be up at the front? It'll cost extra,' a burly, heavily tattooed man said.

'We're fine, wherever,' Isaac said.

'Suit yourself. Up front, the girls get friendly.'

'We should have accepted his offer,' Larry said. 'It seems obvious, our refusing. As if we disapprove.'

'I do.'

'That's not the point. We're here to check out the place, not offer a comment.'

Isaac looked for the man from before. 'Up front,' he said.

'That'll cost you.'

'Okay, put it on the card.'

Hastily moved to the front, the two men sat perilously close to where a woman rotated around a pole. 'It's a meat market,' Isaac said.

'It's where you're meant to be enjoying yourself. You'll have to stop scowling.'

'What if we're recognised?'

'How? I can barely see you in here. The women are well lit, though.'

'You're enjoying this, aren't you?'

'I'm enjoying seeing you squirm. She's not a bad looker, the one on the stage. How much do you reckon? A hundred?'

'Are they all available?'

'Most would be, but Daisy said that Helen wasn't.'

'How could she not be in here?'

'Helen was a rare beauty, everyone's told us that. She's the drawcard, the others are what's available. What did you reckon to Daisy?'

'She's had a tough life.'

'Helen would have if she had stayed here. But then, she was a smart woman. Even if men had not taken her seriously, seen her as a plaything, it's hard to understand what brought her to a place like this.'

The two men's conversation was disturbed by the female from the pole coming in their direction. Larry slipped a five-pound note into her bra; she went away looking for someone more generous. She found him and sat on his lap, continuing to gyrate. Larry watched the action; Isaac pretended not to.

'You don't like the women?' the man from before said.

'Yes, we do,' Isaac said.

'Then don't go skimping on the tips. She's worth more than a measly fiver.'

'It's a rough place,' Isaac said when the man had gone away.

'How can we claim this on expenses?'

'With Richard Goddard, it wouldn't have been a problem. Caddick may not be so easy.'

'It's still a legit expense.'

'Don't worry, he'll sign eventually. His sort of place, I would have thought,' Isaac said.

'What are you going to do about him?'

'We ride out the storm. The man won't last forever.'

'Hey, look at her. She's better than the other one,' Larry said as another female walked onto the stage. Around the two men, the other patrons were clapping.

'Some of them would be in here every night,' Isaac said.

'And around the back.'

'It's not licensed for prostitution.'

'What does it matter? It goes on. These women work on tips, and what they can make on the side. Even then, the management will take a percentage.'

'I still find it hard to believe Helen Langdon worked here.'

'You think there was another side to the woman before she gave up on being an accountant?' Larry said.

'It's possible.'

'We'll check it out.'

'This is not my kind of place,' Isaac said. 'Let's go.'

***

Isaac, not feeling pleased with himself for enjoying the cavorting females at the Dixey Club, although he'd not admit it to his DI, was in the office early the next day. He had dwelt on what they had seen at the club, reflected on the woman that Helen Langdon had been. Isaac was convinced she wasn't as chaste as she had been portrayed.

The team were in the office; Larry, not an early morning person, arrived last.

'We checked out the club last night,' Isaac said.

'Did you enjoy it?' Wendy asked.

'Not particularly,' Isaac said, not wanting to admit the truth. It was as if entry somehow detached the patron from the reality of the outside world. A place where the basest desires were permitted, even encouraged. The men in the audience, what little he had seen of them, had been nudging each other, pointing at the women, making suggestive gestures. The women looked annoyed, yet moved in their direction, allowing them to sample the goods, ensuring that the men stuffed random notes in their underwear.

'Are you going back?' Wendy asked.

'Ben Aberman, any more updates?' Isaac asked.

'I found records of Helen working there, Daisy as well,' Bridget said. 'The dates correlate with Aberman's disappearance, although Helen left two days after the man disappeared. Daisy stayed for another three months.'

'Any more about what Helen did there? From what we could see, all of the women were willing to let the men paw them.'

'Helen must have,' Wendy said.

'Daisy said she didn't and she wasn't into selling herself.'

'Aberman's disappearance and Helen leaving the club two days later is more than a coincidence. Daisy must know more than she told us.'

'We need to talk to her again. Would you like me to deal with it?' Wendy said.

'Take her for a meal. She looked as though she could do with one. Talk to her woman to woman,' Isaac said.

'I know what to do, guv.'

'Aberman's house, do you have an address, Bridget?'

'It's in the country. I'll give it to you.'

***

'What do you hope to gain from this?' Larry said as he and Isaac drove out to Aberman's house.

'Helen Langdon's story is a lie. As though she orchestrated this whole subterfuge.'

'But why?'

'I don't know, and that concerns me. If she could maintain a cover for so long, what else is she capable of?'

'Gerald Adamant?'

'What if she did kill him, and not in self-defence?' Isaac said.

'The woman admitted to killing him. She served time in prison.'

'She was even the one who phoned the police to give herself up, which tends to destroy my argument.'

'I can see what you're getting at,' Larry said. 'Ben Aberman.'

'What if she killed him? We don't know how and why, and maybe it's a red herring.'

'If she's working in the club, and the men are keeping their distance, and she's not selling herself, it can only mean one thing.'

'She was Aberman's woman.'

'Too many loose ends. She was an accountant, a reputable firm. No doubt she was annoyed with all the attention, the lewd comments, but she was a smart woman, and there are laws in this country. She could have done something about it, other than take off her business suit and gyrate around a pole, and what if some of her former clients or former work colleagues came in?'

Aberman's house, better than expected, sat on the edge of the village. Larry got out of the car and opened the gate for Isaac to drive in. An old lady appeared from one side of the house. 'What are you doing here? I'll call the police.'

'We are the police,' Larry said. 'We're following up on Mr Aberman's disappearance.'

'I'll need to see your identification.'

'No problems. And you are?'

'I live next door. I keep a watch on the house for Mr Aberman.'

'He's been missing for a long time.'

'A woman comes here sometimes. She gives me some money for my trouble.'

'How often?' Isaac said, having joined Larry and the old lady outside the front door of the house.

'Sometimes she phones, but every month some money, not that I need it.'

'When was the last time you saw Mr Aberman?'

'It's a few years. He's overseas.'

'What can you tell us about him?'

'He used to come here most weekends. He was always pleasant to me, always brought some flowers or chocolates. He worked in London.'

'Do you know what sort of business?'

'He said he was in the entertainment business. That explained some of the people I saw here.'

'What sort of people?'

'Show business types, expensive cars, fur coats, parties on the lawn at the back.'

'And then he left?'

'One day he's here, the next he's gone. I thought it strange at the time as he always came over to my house to say goodbye. He was a gentleman. And then a woman turns up, tells me he's travelling, and would I look after the house. Not that there's much to do. A man comes once a month to mow the lawn, and I dust inside the best I can, but that's about it.'

'Can you describe the woman?'

'Laura. An attractive woman, younger than him.'

'Was she here most weekends?'

'Not always, and then she disappeared for a few years, but the money still came through.'

Isaac looked at Larry, knew what he was thinking.

'It's important,' Isaac said. 'Can you describe this woman in detail?'

'She looked no older than my granddaughter, and she's not yet thirty. She spoke nicely, always very polite.'

'When was the last time you saw her?'

'Two weeks ago.'

'Her car?'

'She didn't drive. There's a railway station here, and it's not far to walk.'

'I've a photo. Can you tell me if it is her?' Isaac said as he handed the woman the picture.

The old woman took out her glasses from the pocket of the coat she was wearing, Isaac and Larry were champing at the bit, waiting for an answer. The woman took her time.

'Yes, that's her. That's Laura, such a nice person. Or I think it is. She dresses differently when she comes here, more sombre. She always has dark sunglasses on, never takes them off, not even when she comes in my house for a cup of tea. A lovely person, and so was Mr Aberman. I hope he'll be back soon.'

Chapter 9

Wendy arrived outside Daisy's flat at nine in the morning. If the woman had been working at night, she would be asleep, not that it would discourage Wendy from knocking. The flat, three floors up and with no lift, proved difficult for the police sergeant.

Where Daisy lived was not affluent, not for someone who could make five hundred pounds in one night, but then, Daisy, like a lot of the other women selling their wares on a street corner or in a club, had a problem. It had been clear when the woman was at Challis Street Police Station that she was a drug addict, the worst kind.

Wendy knocked on the door, more firmly the second time. A woman poked her head out from a door opposite. 'There's a key under the mat,' she said. Wendy could see the block of flats catered to the ladies of the night.

'Thank you.' Wendy bent down, steadying herself on the wall in front of her. She picked up the key and inserted it into the lock. Inside the flat were signs of neglect: unwashed dishes, a cat that looked as if it was in need of a feed, a discarded syringe. Wendy moved through the flat, opening the first bedroom door. A woman, semi-comatose, briefly stirred. 'Close the door, I'm trying to sleep.'

'Sorry,' Wendy said. She moved on through the flat, stepping over a pile of discarded clothes. She opened one door to find out it was the bathroom, its condition the same as the rest of the flat. The third door, where she gently knocked before entering, was slightly ajar.

On the bed, Wendy could see the form of a woman under the blankets. 'Daisy, it's Sergeant Gladstone,' she said.

With no sign of movement, Wendy moved closer to the bed. She pulled back the blanket, then picked up her phone and dialled Isaac. 'There's another one,' she said.

'Daisy?'

'Not long by the looks of it.'

You know the procedure. We'll be there as soon as we can.'

Wendy phoned Gordon Windsor, the CSE. 'One hour, secure the location,' he said.

With the crime scene investigation team on their way, Wendy phoned for two uniforms to come to the flat and establish a crime scene. She then went into the other room where Daisy's flatmate was asleep and nudged her to wake up.

'Go away. Can't you see I'm asleep?'

'Sergeant Wendy Gladstone, Challis Street Police Station. Your sleep will need to wait.'

The woman stirred after Wendy had prodded her two more times, receiving a few expletives in return. Finally, she stood up, naked, and Wendy could see the woman was similar to Daisy: the gaunt frame, the result of drugs rather than food, the needle marks, the blotched body. Reaching for a top and a skirt, the woman turned to face Wendy. 'Did you get a good look?' she said.

'Nothing that interests me. Did you hear what I said before?'

'Something about the police.'

'That's correct. Sergeant Wendy Gladstone. I need you out of this flat.'

'What for? I've done nothing wrong.'

'Apart from selling yourself and jamming needles in your arm, you've probably not. Besides, I'm not here about you.'

'Then what do you want?'

'Your flatmate, Daisy. She's dead in the other room.'

'Oh.'

'Is that all you've got to say?'

'What do you want me to say? She was going to OD sometime. The same as me, I suppose.'

'She did not OD, she was murdered,' Wendy said.

'Who'd do that?'

Unable to do anything more with the woman, Wendy grabbed a coat from the back of the woman's door, took her by one arm, and moved her out of the flat, avoiding the traffic areas as much as possible. A uniform was coming up the stairs. 'I'll take it from here,' he said.

Downstairs, Wendy put the woman in her car and turned on the heater. 'Stay here, I'll be back.'

'Don't worry about me. I've still got some sleeping to do.'

Isaac and Larry had arrived. Wendy went over to where they were parked. 'Was she shot?' Isaac asked.

'Not this time. There's a cord around her neck.'

'The flatmate?'

'She's in my car. A herd of elephants could have gone through the flat. She wouldn't have heard anything.'

'We'll need to interview her.'

'Here or at Challis Street?'

'Challis Street. She can't go back into the flat, and there's nowhere else.'

'There's another woman in the flat opposite. We'll need to talk to her.'

'We'll deal with it,' Larry said. 'Find out what you can from the flatmate.'

Gordon Windsor arrived. 'Have you been in?' he said.

'Wendy found the body,' Isaac said.

'Have you touched anything?' Windsor said to Wendy.

'No more than was necessary. The flatmate's in my car.'

'I'll send someone to take her prints. We've got yours on file.'

'There's a woman in the flat opposite that we need to question,' Isaac said.

'Go ahead, but wear foot protectors, gloves outside of the woman's flat. There may be some evidence on the landing. Professional, was it?' Windsor said as he kitted up, preparing to enter the building.

'There's been no violence, no sign of the place being disrupted, although that's not so easy to tell.'

'The woman?'

'A prostitute. We interviewed her at Challis Street the other day.'

'Not another of your murder enquiries where the bodies keep piling up, is it? You may as well let me know so I can arrange extra personnel.'

'There'll be more,' Isaac said. 'Larry, kit up. We need to talk to the neighbour.'

Wendy left the men and walked back to her car. The flatmate was fast asleep in the back seat. Wendy opened the door, and the woman woke up with a start. 'This man needs to take your fingerprints. We need to eliminate you from the crime.'

'What crime?'

'Your flatmate, Daisy.'

'What about her?'

'She's dead. I told you before. Someone's killed her.'

'It wasn't me.'

'We know that, but the crime scene examiners need to eliminate your prints when they're checking the flat.'

'What about me?'

'We'll go to the police station. We'll have a chat, and then I'll see that you have accommodation. I'll also make sure you get some food.'

'It's not food I want.'

'That I can't supply. If it becomes an issue, we'll bring in a doctor.'

***

Isaac and Larry climbed the stairs to the neighbour's flat. Her door was open on their arrival, a police constable barring the woman from leaving. 'He won't let me out,' she said.

'A few questions and then we'll make sure you can leave.'

'I've got to work.'

'What do you do?'

'Not what they were up to. I've got a job. A place that makes meat pies.'

'Any good?' Larry said.

'I'll eat them, doubt if they'll serve them up in a fancy restaurant.'

'Can we come in?' Isaac said.

'What about my job?'

'Can you phone, tell them you'll be in late?'

'I've no credit on my phone, and the phone in here doesn't work.'

'You can use my phone,' Isaac said.

'Don't worry, it'll be fine. You better come in.'

The two men entered the flat. It was tidy, even if the paint was peeling, but there was a distinct smell of sewage emanating from the bathroom.

'I do my best,' the woman said, 'but the landlord, he doesn't care.'

'You've got a lease and a number for a plumber. Phone him up.'

'The landlord, he'll make an excuse, have me out of here in a minute.'

'Using a property without the owner's permission for the purpose of prostitution invalidates the lease. That's the reason you don't phone him up.'

'I don't like to advertise what I do. That's why I use the meat pie story.'

'Your name?' Isaac said.

'Hailey Ashmore.'

Isaac studied the woman. She certainly looked better than Daisy had that day in Challis Street, and there were no signs of drug use. Her manner, apart from at the door, was calm.

'Busy, are you?' Larry said.

'I do what's necessary. Life's not always fair.'

'We're here to investigate the death of Elizabeth Wetherington, also known as Daisy.'

'She was always going to come to a sticky end.'

'Why?'

'She's out at all hours, and then she has the occasional man over. I can hear them going at it from here.'

'No doubt they can hear you.'

'Not me. My clients, they're special.'

Isaac knew they were not. Special clients do not visit rundown flats that smell of sewage and cheap perfume.

'Did you see or hear anything last night?'

'Not me.'

'On your own?'

'Don't ask me his name.'

'Why?'

'I don't know it.'

'You're occupied for thirty minutes, and then he leaves.'

'I give my men a good time. It's more than a quick screw with me and out of the door. You're a good-looking man, I could give you a special rate.'

'We're here to discuss Daisy. How well did you know her?'

'Not that well. We'd talk outside on the landing, sometimes.'

'Her flatmate?'

'Gwendoline, she calls herself. You'd think she was a fairy with a name like that. A right tart.'

'Why do you call her a tart? You're here selling yourself.'

'Daisy was bad enough, but her flatmate is worse.'

'What do you mean?'

'I was coming back here one night with a gentleman friend, and there she was on the stairs, her skirt hitched up around her arse, a drunk going for dear life. My friend, he wanted to leave, but I made him come in, gave him a special treat.'

Isaac did not want to hear what the special treat was. 'Last night, when you weren't taking one of your gentlemen friends to paradise and back, did you hear anything unusual?'

'Not me. I've no idea what time the two of them came home, or who they were with. That's the honest truth.'

Both Isaac and Larry weren't convinced they had been told the full truth, but there was no more to be gained in the flat, and the smell was becoming nauseous. 'We'll take you out of here if you want,' Larry said.

'Don't bother. I've got someone coming over later.'

***

At the police station, Wendy sat with Gwendoline. A café across
the road had sent over a full English breakfast, which the flatmate
was devouring as if she hadn't eaten a decent meal for a long
time.

'Gwendoline, what's your real name?' Wendy asked.

'Kate Bellamy.'

'Your age?'

'Is this necessary?'

'I'm afraid it is. You were in the flat when your flatmate
was murdered.'

'I didn't kill her.'

'We've discounted you for the present. What can you tell
us about last night?'

'Not a lot. It was a quiet night, just a couple of men.'

'Barely enough to pay the rent?'

'It'll be better tonight, but now I've got to find
somewhere to live.'

'Do you have anywhere?'

'One of the other women on the street, she's looking for
someone to share.'

'And the flat where you are now?'

'It was in Daisy's name. I just paid my share. The
landlord's not going to have much success claiming the rent from
her.'

'He may ask you to pay.'

'If he's a nuisance, I'll pay him off.'

'With money?'

'What do you think?'

Wendy had found in Daisy a vulnerable person destroyed
by drugs. She wasn't so sure of Gwendoline. The woman was a
drug addict, her arms testament to the fact, but with a full
stomach, she was no longer showing the signs of severe
addiction.

'Daisy was killed, which means someone must have entered your flat, walked along the hallway outside of your door, killed her, and then walked past your door again on the way out.'

'What do you want me to say?'

'I want you to tell me the truth. I want to know if you heard anything?'

'Sometimes Daisy has someone over. Sometimes I do. We mind each other's business. There was a noise, about two in the morning.'

'How do you know the time.'

'I'm giving you the facts I can remember. Whether they're accurate or not, I wouldn't know.'

'Why not?'

'Daisy and me, we're night owls. When it's dark, we go out to work. I had come home early for once, but I'm going nowhere, and besides, I'm not feeling so good.'

'Any reason?'

'I don't feel good a lot of times.'

'You've seen a doctor?'

'What for? He'll only tell me what to do.'

'And what's wrong with that?'

'I've got to earn a living. I don't have time for healthy food and exercise, and I'm not going to get off my back and find an honest job.'

'Is it better to have a sweaty man on top of you than a regular job?'

'The money's better.'

'The way you live doesn't show it.'

'Maybe it doesn't, but I've got a problem.'

'The same as Daisy, heroin.'

'She was crazy for it. I'm not so bad. If someone had snuck into her room last night, she wouldn't have known.'

'How would they have got into the flat?'

'How did you?'

'The key under the mat.'

'Sometimes we come home, can't remember w key is, sometimes without a handbag.'

'Why?'

'Some of the men, they aren't so good. They d to pay, see us as tarts, and either they hit us, or they tak handbags, phones, as well.'

'Rough life?'

'You get used to it. What else do you want? I sa did nothing. Daisy's dead, she's not the first one that's d

'What do you mean?'

'Drugs. It'll kill me eventually.'

'I could get treatment for you.'

'Don't bother. I need to get into my room, get my clothes.'

'I'll take you back, and then take you where you want to go.'

'The police, they're not like you. Some of them move us on, some of them take liberties.'

'They'd be liable to internal discipline if they were discovered.'

'Don't worry. I'll not tell you who they are.'

70

Chapter 10

Seth Caddick sat in his office and looked out of the window. His conversation with Commissioner Davies had left him perplexed. He knew the man would not protect him, and it was up to him to secure his position. He enjoyed the rank of detective superintendent, and that everyone called him sir, except Isaac Cook, who was liable to forget.

'Chloe,' he called out through the open door. Caddick's secretary came in.

'You wanted me,' she said. Caddick had brought her in from his previous station. The opportunity to appoint someone local had been there, but who in the Met could be trusted. Chloe, he knew, was as loyal to him as she was to her job.

'Wendy Gladstone. We've got to remove Cook's support mechanism.'

'A medical?'

'When's it due?'

'Two months.'

'Bring it forward. Four weeks' time, and then I want her retired due to health reasons.'

'You'll need to give her notice of the medical.'

'Then do it today and make the appointment. I want a full check-up, no letting her pass because she's getting old. After that, we'll go for Larry Hill. He's not looking so good.'

'He looks fine to me,' Chloe said.

'He was badly beaten before. It must have had some effect.'

'Can't you just remove DCI Cook?'

'It's better to follow the procedure, and besides, I need him to wrap up the murder of James Holden.'

'And the women who've been killed.'

'Two whores. They don't matter.'

'Be careful. Helen Langdon was well connected.'

'How? She murdered Adamant, bedded Saint Holden, destroyed his reputation. There'll not be much interest in her.'

***

James Holden had been a complicated man. A man whose inner demons tormented him, the occasional urge to give in to temptation. Violet, his wife, had recognised it early in their marriage; she had decided not to allow it to destroy the love she had for the man, the inherent goodness in him.

After the first time, and each and every time after that, he had come to her and confessed. Not that she wanted to hear, but she knew that with honesty comes respect, even love. And now the facts were out. He had been with another woman, a now-dead prostitute by the name of Daisy, and there it was, emblazoned across the television. She had seen the black policeman, Isaac Cook, waylaid on his way out of the building where the woman had died. His inability to avoid making a statement, offering the usual platitudes: unable to make a comment at this stage, investigations are ongoing, charges will be laid soon.

Violet wondered who the charges would be laid against. Would it be her son? He had the anger, but why a prostitute of no importance? And there was Helen. She had a past history, and somehow it was tied to this other woman. It concerned Violet, having seen her son John's fits of violence as a child, the pulling off of a butterfly's wings, the senseless killing of a cat that had strayed into the garden, the embarrassment of explaining to the neighbours that she and James were not sure where they had gone wrong.

Violet remembered John's anger when Helen had rejected him. She realised the signs were there all along, the glances between James and Helen, brushing against each other in the office, the whispered conversations. She had wanted to confront her husband, but she had not. After all, hadn't he been honest in the past. And now, the man was dead, as was Helen. Was it the first time James had slept with Helen? Violet thought, and why

72

had Helen not wanted her son? He was a man more her age, a man who would have given Helen children, yet the woman had wanted older men, men with one foot in the grave. Men who would die from a hammer blow to the head, and now from a bullet. If Helen had not died, Violet would have thought her responsible for James's demise. It could not be her, but it could be John. She hoped it was not.

***

'Aberman's next-door neighbour identified Helen Langdon,' Isaac said. It was 6 a.m. in the office, a good time for Isaac to lay out the plan for the day, not so good for the others.

'Inconclusive, guv. The neighbour is getting on a bit, and any woman covered up could have been mistaken for Helen Langdon,' Larry said.

'That's why we're not placing emphasis on it for the present moment, and where's the tie-in?'

'Wendy, apart from your medical, what have you got?'

'I can't pass it, and you know it.'

'You will. You're on an exercise routine. We'll get you fit. How's your blood pressure, lung capacity?'

'Fine. I had myself checked out a few months back, no serious damage. It's arthritis, that's what it is. I just can't move as fast as before.'

'Fast enough for this department.'

'It's our superintendent, isn't it?' Wendy said.

'He's weakening my base, going for the kill,' Isaac said.

'You don't intend to let him win, do you?'

'Not this time. We fight fire with fire. How's your health, Bridget?'

'Fine, but I'm not up for a medical.'

'Every morning, you've got to take a one-hour walk with Wendy, and easy on the food. No more hamburgers, greasy chips. From now on, it's salads and eating healthily, chicken if you're desperate.'

'Me, as well?'

'Bridget, you're to set Wendy an example.'

'Don't worry, Wendy. We'll get you through this,' Bridget said to her friend.

A period of magnanimity existed in the office, only to be disturbed by Caddick coming in the door. 'DCI, what's going on?'

'We'll talk later,' Isaac said to his team.

'One more murder. Is that right?' Caddick said as he sat down on a chair in Isaac's office.

'We know the woman had been an acquaintance of Helen Langdon.'

'Did she kill Langdon and Holden?'

'She's not involved.'

'Then why has she been killed?'

'It was in my report.'

'Too busy last night to read it. Give me the shortened version,' Caddick said.

That's what I gave you, you pompous fool, Isaac thought. Instead, he said, 'Before Helen Langdon married Gerald Adamant, she worked in a club.'

'What sort?'

'Gentlemen's.'

'Strip joint?'

'Yes.'

'Call it what it is. Don't go giving me the benefit of your fancy education. A spade is a spade, a place where the women prance around with nothing on is a strip joint. Do I make myself clear?'

'Yes, you do.'

'And it's sir to you. Your insubordination is wearing thin. I've put up with it till now on account of your past record. Dismal to me, but there are others who think you're special. And as for your staff...'

'Are you about to launch into a tirade about them?'

'A critical observation. They're a tired bunch of individuals, not worthy of feeding.'

'Sir, you, as a detective superintendent, must realise that derogatory remarks about personnel are an actionable offence. You could be reported for what you've just said.'

'Just you try it, Cook.'

'I intend to register a formal complaint against you in line with regulations.'

'I'll have you out of here in an instant.'

'Not while the complaint is ongoing, you won't. You'll have to give your reasons, and believe me, you'll not win.'

'Cook, it's you or me.'

'That's fine by me. Let's see how you get out of this one.'

'Do you want to make a comment here about me?' Caddick said.

'Not a chance. We'll wait until the hearing into my complaint comes up.'

'Is this how you spoke to Goddard?'

'Detective Chief Superintendent Goddard was a competent man. It wasn't necessary.'

'And I'm not?'

'I've nothing more to say. If you have no more to add to our conversation, I'll wish you goodbye. I've got three murders to solve.'

After Caddick had left, red in the face, Larry came into Isaac's office. 'You've made a cross for yourself to bear. Was it wise?'

'Probably not.'

***

The Dixey Club did not appreciate a visit from Homicide. It was still early in the evening, a few hours before the entertainment began. Isaac was pleased the lights were on. At the back door of the club, which opened onto an alley, two uniforms had been stationed in case someone wanted to slip out.

'You can't come in here,' the burly man from Isaac and Larry's previous visit said.

'DCI Cook. I've got a warrant.'

'We're clean, nothing to see here.'

'We've got a few questions. Is the manager here?'

'I'm the manager.'

'No, you're not. He's got an office out the back. We'll find him.'

Wendy walked through the place, saw the pole in the middle of the stage, walked through a door behind it, found some women in early for the night's entertainment. 'Sergeant Wendy Gladstone,' she said.

'We've done nothing wrong,' one of the women said. Wendy had seen the photos of the ladies on display outside: beautiful, fresh and young, and one of them of a more youthful Helen. Those preparing themselves were not. They didn't have much in the way of clothing, although one was dressed as a cowgirl, another as a nurse. The third, Wendy was not sure what she was meant to represent, but it looked weird to her.

'I'm not saying you have, but I've a few questions.'

Wendy could see the women were nervous.

'I'm not here for you three. If you've committed any crime, that's not my interest. There were a couple of women who worked here some years ago.'

'I've only been here two,' the youngest of the three said.

'Maybe you don't know. How about you?' Wendy said, looking at one of the girls, although she was well over thirty, probably closer to forty.

'I've been here a while. Who do you want to know about?'

'One was Daisy. The other one was named …'

'Helen, that's who you mean, isn't it?'

'Yes. What do you know about them?'

The woman dressed as a cowgirl, straightened herself on her chair. 'Daisy, she was game for anything.'

'Explain "game",' Wendy said.

'The men, they get carried away, wanting to do things they're not meant to.'

'Such as?'

'Exposing themselves, grabbing too much of us.'

'It's on display,' Wendy said.

'So's the meat at the butchers, but you don't go prodding it.'

'Do you object?'

'Not if they're paying and it remains light-hearted, but some of the men, well, you know?'

'I don't. I've not frequented these places.'

The youngest of the three spoke. Wendy realised she was dressed as an astronaut, although not from NASA. 'Some of them, they think because we strip on the stage, let them take a few liberties, that we're prostitutes, available to the highest tipper.'

'Aren't you?'

'Sometimes we'll negotiate a special deal, but we'll not do it on the stage or in the audience. We've some standards.'

'Daisy?'

'She was always available. She could have made herself plenty of money, apart from her addiction.'

'And you three?'

'I was into drugs a few years back,' the eldest said. The other two are clean.'

'So why be here?'

'Life's expensive, you know that,' the youngest said. 'I can make more here in two days than working all week in a regular job.'

'So how many days do you work here?'

'Four, and sometimes a Saturday.'

'Which means?'

'The rest of the week is free.'

'To do what?'

'There are one or two men.'

'Escort?'

'They pay plenty. I'm buying myself a flat, putting myself through university.'

'Are there beds out back?'

'Are you here to arrest us?'

'I'm with Homicide. We deal with murders, not who you screw on the premises.'

'Sometimes it happens,' the oldest of the three said.

'I'm not involved, I've got my men to consider. They don't want the goods damaged,' the youngest one said.

'Okay, enough about you three and this place, what about Daisy and Helen?'

'Daisy, she'd play the men, let them go further than they should. Sometimes, the management wanted her to go easy, but she was a drawcard, the same as Helen.'

'How?'

'Daisy, she's the rough, Helen, she's the pure. Helen, she'd get the men excited, playing to the crowd, teasing them, pulling back. Once they've lined up a likely mark, Daisy would come along, make sure the man or men were stuffing plenty of money into whatever she was wearing. Later Daisy would take them around the back and fleece some more money out of them.'

'Helen?'

'Never in this club. She played her part, that was all, and she was good.'

'Did you like her?'

'Everyone liked Helen, and now she's dead.'

'So is Daisy.'

'Daisy was always going to end up that way.'

'You knew about Helen marrying, and then killing her husband?'

'We knew.'

'What did you think?'

'She wasn't the sort of person to kill anyone.'

'But she could strut herself here, bait the men.'

'It doesn't make us all murderers, does it?'

'I'm trying to understand the woman.'

'Mind you, her becoming involved with Ben Aberman was not expected.'

'Why?'

'Aberman, he owned this place.'

'And he disappeared,' Wendy said. 'What's the full story?'

'Helen wanted more than this club. She told us she wanted to find a decent man to look after her.'

'A sugar daddy?'

'Not Helen. She was good at detaching herself. In here, she'd play the tart, outside she'd not want to associate with us.'

'What can you tell us about Ben Aberman?'

'He was a rogue, but he was a decent man, and he treated the girls with respect.'

'Were they living together?'

'We knew Helen would spend the night with him sometimes, and he was really keen on her.'

'And Helen?'

'She said she didn't love him, and it was just a business partnership.'

'What do you think she meant?'

'No idea really. She wasn't even escorting, and she could have made plenty of money. We never really understood why she was here.'

'Aberman disappeared,' Wendy said.

'We were told he went overseas.'

'And Helen's reaction?'

'She was ambivalent, told us not to worry, and that he would turn up in a few days.'

'And then Helen left.'

'Two days later, she's gone, never even said goodbye.'

'Did you look for her?'

'We did for a few days, but she'd left where she was living, never left a forwarding address. We assumed she was with Ben, but then, not long afterwards, she lands herself a rich man and marries him.'

'Did you ever speak to her again?'

'None of us did. She was the one that got away.'

Chapter 11

Out front in the club, the manager stood with Isaac and Larry. 'Ben Aberman, before my time,' he said. 'Sorry, can't help you.'

Isaac had met his type before: only interested in a profit, not caring how it was earned.'

'Your name?'

'Barry Knox.'

'You're soliciting on these premises. We know it, so do you. What do you want? This place to be closed down, or do you want to cooperate?'

'I'll need my lawyer here.'

'That's up to you, but you're opening up in sixty minutes. You'd better get him here fast.'

'You can't close me down.'

'You're up to your neck in crime. I was here the other night with DI Hill. We saw what was going on.'

'Harmless fun.'

'Are you dealing in drugs here?'

'We're clean. The place is legit, more than I can say for two undercover police officers casing the joint.'

'It's called policing. If you try it on us, I'll haul you down the police station and throw you in a cell for the night.'

'You can't talk to Mr Knox like that,' the tattooed man, who had been there on Isaac and Larry's first visit to the club, said.

'We can. And as for you, back off,' Isaac said. 'Do you have a record, been involved in any crime lately? And what do you know about this place, have you taken any liberties with the women?'

'You've no right.'

'I've every right. I need answers as to what happened to Ben Aberman, and what about Helen and Daisy, and don't make out you don't know who I'm referring to. Men like you don't move far. You would have been here then, so would your manager, or if he wasn't, he'd know people who were, people who know the true story.'

'Okay, you've made your point,' Knox said. 'It's best if you come into my office.'

The four men walked the short distance to the office. In the room, a monitor showed the stage, another showed the patrons, and another the room where the women gave the patrons individual attention.

'You've got a licence for that?' Isaac asked, pointing to the bed in the bare room.

'It's our first aid room,' Knox said.

'Knox, you'd better start talking.'

'Ben Aberman, I knew him, so did Gus. He wasn't pulling in the money, and his lenders were anxious. I came in to run the place and make it financially sound.'

'The lenders?'

'You don't go to the bank to open a strip club.'

'Loan sharks?'

'Businessmen. It's all legal. Aberman signed the documents, agreed to the terms and conditions.'

'Back then, you had Helen and Daisy, the double act. This place must have been making money.'

'Maybe it was, or maybe Aberman was creaming more off the top than he should have.'

'Which is it?'

'Aberman, he owned this place, but he wasn't honest with his financial backers, delaying the repayments.'

'Are you one of the backers?'

'Not me. I'm just the person sent in to make it pay.'

'Is it now?'

'We get by.'

'Which means it is, but you don't declare it.'

'Inspector Cook, we're a business. We make money, we spend money. How we structure our finances is not your concern. You're after Aberman, am I correct?'

'What about Gus here? What's he got to do with Aberman?'

'I did nothing with the man. He was my friend,' Gus said.

'Where's Aberman?' Isaac asked.

'I don't know, and that's the honest truth.'

'We know that Aberman does not own this club. Was the signing over of the business legal, or was his arm bent?'

'I wouldn't know. I'm just the humble manager,' Knox said.

'Did Gus force Aberman to sign the business over. What had Aberman been subjected to before he signed? What happened afterwards?'

'Aberman, he was reluctant, but they wanted to get their money. I'll swear on my mother's grave that nothing happened to him.'

'I pity your mother if she's dead. Aberman, he's forced to sign, and then he's dumped in a river somewhere, or taken out to sea. Did he cry when you threw him over the side?' Isaac said.

'You've got this all wrong. Aberman's out of the country.'

'Where?'

'He doesn't send me postcards. Helen, she knew.'

'She's dead, so is Daisy. Mr Knox, there are too many coincidences pointing back to this place and to you. And why did Helen leave the club two days after Aberman vanished, Daisy within three months?'

'She didn't want to work here without Aberman, and Daisy, we got rid of her in the end.'

'That's probably the first truthful answer you've given. Daisy was a hopeless drug addict, probably too much for even this club to handle. Helen, why two days? Did she know the story, did you pay her off?'

'I've told you the truth. What more do you want from me?'

'Was Helen involved with Aberman?'

'They were cosy.'

'Sleeping together?'

'Aberman was a snake.'

'So why was Helen with him?'

'I don't know. You could have asked her if she was alive.'

'Do you and your kind have any decency left in you? You killed Aberman, but you couldn't kill Helen. We know of her hold over men. Did she have it over you? Did she have it over Gus?'

'Helen was not as good as you make her out to be. Helen and Aberman made a good team, and then he's not around, and Helen's out of here in two days. We paid her up, it's in the books.'

'Aberman's house?'

'What about it?'

'If the man's got debts and the loan sharks...'

'They're businessmen, tough businessmen,' Knox corrected Isaac.

'Okay, have it your way,' Isaac said. 'These businessmen would not have allowed Aberman's house to remain in his name. They would have wanted it as security.'

'If they knew about it.'

'They did. The man had parties there. Parties attended by the cream, sour probably, of the criminal classes.'

'There was an agreement,' Knox said. 'If Aberman gave the clubs he owned over to them willingly, then the debt was absolved.'

'And where does Helen come into this?'

'Aberman made it clear she was to have the house if she wanted it.'

'But it's in Aberman's name.'

'Which proves he's still alive, paying the bills.'

'Why did he want to let Helen have the house?'

'Aberman was a sentimental fool. He'd fallen in love with the woman, the same as that old man she married, the same as that old fool she was shot with.'

'Was Helen capable of love?'

'I wouldn't know. She was a beautiful woman, but she never came near me.'

'Why?'

'Look at me. The manager of a strip joint.'

'So was Aberman.'

'Was he? The man had more than a few interests around here. He had plenty of money.'

'Then why not pay his debts?'

'He didn't get the money in the first place by giving it away.'

'Aberman's dead,' Isaac said. 'We'll find out what happened to him. In the interim, I'd suggest you tone down your activities here. Otherwise, there'll be another raid, and the police won't be walking out of here empty-handed.'

***

'Look at this,' Isaac said, pushing the opened letter across his desk to Larry. The two had just returned to Challis Street after visiting the Dixey Club.

'Are you surprised?'

'Not even a warning. I'm to present myself in two weeks for a disciplinary hearing.'

'DCS Goddard can't get you out of this.'

'I should have been more careful with Caddick, but the man's a bore. He doesn't know what he's talking about half the time, and the other half, he's sucking up to Davies.'

'What will you do?'

'I'll mount a vigorous defence.'

'It'll not work, and you know it. You told him what you thought of him, didn't you?'

'I did, and he's kept out of the way for a few days. No doubt working overtime on setting up my impending demise.'

'That serious?'

'They have the power to stand me down.'

'They could do that now.'

'Not Caddick. He wants these murders solved. That's why he's going for two weeks. He's hoping we'll be close by then, and he can step in and take the glory.'

'What about us?' Larry said.

'Solving these murders is always the best defence.'

'You were shot in the shoulder once before, got a medal,' Larry said.

'Are you suggesting I do that again?'

'Desperate times demand desperate measures.'

'Okay, Larry, enough of your jokes. What did we reckon of Barry Knox?'

'We should call in Bridget and Wendy.'

With the four in the office, Isaac took control. 'Bridget, what do we have on Barry Knox?'

'Minor hooligan. He's been arrested for pimping, spent six months in prison before getting out on a technicality.'

'Technicality?'

'The arresting officer had falsified some entries in his notes. Apart from that, Barry Knox is clean. He's managed a few clubs in the area, mostly seedy, and he's been at Dixey's since Aberman disappeared.'

'And the women at the club, Wendy?'

'One or two convictions against the oldest two for prostitution, nothing against the other woman.'

'Why's that?'

'A sign of the times. The young woman is studying for a degree and paying off a mortgage. She needs the money, and casual work in a shop or with a catering company doesn't pay the bills. She can get up on that stage, makes a few hundred for the night and survive.'

'Escorting?'

'Probably. They were honest about Helen and Daisy, gave some insights about Aberman.'

'Gus, the heavy?'

'According to the women, he's not too bright, but loyal, polite to the women, never takes advantage, although he's always peering into the changing room.'

'He'll see more on the stage, and Knox has a camera on the bed at the rear of the building. Which of your women were using it?'

'They weren't willing to admit it to me. The oldest one would be the most likely, but I've no proof.'

'Don't worry. We're after a murderer or murderers, not fallen women. Aberman, any luck finding him, Bridget? And if it was Helen, who was paying for the electricity, the rates, why was the house empty?'

'The rates are paid from an account in London,' Bridget said. 'There's a solicitor's firm that's taken responsibility.'

'The address?'

'It's in your inbox.'

'Larry, let's go,' Isaac said.

'Don't you want to stay and prepare your defence,' Larry said.

'Defence? Wendy said.

'I'm up before a disciplinary hearing,' Isaac said. 'Don't worry about it. You focus on passing your medical. I can deal with our superintendent. And get Gordon Windsor and his crime scene team primed to check out Aberman's house.'

'You don't think…?'

'I don't think anything at the present moment, but Helen Langdon's been murdered for a reason, as has James Holden. What if it's to do with Aberman's disappearance? Maybe Helen did love James Holden, told him her story. The man wasn't judgemental, no reason to be, but with Adamant, she was always careful.'

Chapter 12

'Can I help?' a polite young woman said from behind her desk. The firm of Slaters and Partners occupied two offices on the fourth floor of an office block in Mayfair.

'Detective Chief Inspector Cook, Detective Inspector Hill. We'd like to talk to one of the senior partners,' Isaac said.

'Mr Slater is in. I'll let him know you're here. You don't have an appointment, I suppose?'

'We're here on official business.'

'Please take a seat. I'm sure he won't be long.'

The two men settled on a leather sofa in the corner of the reception area. 'Attractive,' Larry said.

'I didn't notice.'

'Come off it. You're on your own again. It can't be much fun.'

'I've got you and Homicide,' Isaac said. 'What more could I want?'

'And Caddick for the argumentative mother-in-law.'

'My life is complete.' Isaac realised the relationship with his DI had become more cordial in recent months.

'Mr Slater will see you now,' the lady at reception said.

Isaac and Larry entered Slater's office. 'Always pleased to meet members of our fine police force. What I can do for you.'

'There's a property in the village of Bray. It's a two-storey, three- or four-bedroom house. It's been unoccupied for some years.

'Mr Aberman's house?'

'That's it.'

'What do you want to know?'

'We need to contact Mr Aberman.'

'I can't help you there.'

'You do pay the bills for the place?'

'That's correct. I have sufficient funds deposited in a trust account to cover the bills.'

'Did Mr Aberman set it up?'

'Yes, just before he went overseas.'

'Have you spoken to him since.'

'There's been no reason to. The instructions were clear. The house was to be maintained, the rates were to be paid, and a small account set up, with a debit card sent to a nominated address.'

'And you never queried this?'

'I've no reason to. London, especially the better areas, is awash with empty houses, absent landlords. My instructions were clear, and I've carried them out to the best of my ability.'

'You mentioned a debit card?'

'Yes. The balance of the account is kept at one thousand pounds.'

'Do you have an address for the card?'

'I've always sent it to a post office box.'

'Is that unusual?'

'A little strange, I'll grant you. Some people are reclusive, or they do not want their identities revealed. As long as I conduct my business according to the law, then I have no reason to concern myself.'

'You must be curious,' Larry said.

'Why? If Mr Aberman wants to act in a certain way, then I don't interfere.'

'Two people he knew have been murdered. We suspect Aberman has been as well. We need to prove our suspicion. Have you ever met a Helen Langdon or a Helen Mackay?'

'No.'

'You seem certain.'

'I watch the news. I'm aware that a Helen Langdon was found dead with James Holden. I take it that is the woman you're referring to.'

'It is.'

'Then I've not met her, not even spoken to her.'

***

It took a few days before all the paperwork was in place. The notification had been given to Slater, Aberman's solicitor, and Ben Aberman's next-door neighbour had been informed.

Four vehicles stood in the driveway of Aberman's house, with a uniform out on the street to deal with the onlookers. 'Just routine,' if anyone asked them.

Gordon Windsor walked around the house with Isaac, Slater having given them a key. 'It's musty in here,' Windsor said.

'What will you find in here?'

'No idea. The garden interests us more. We've got a couple of ground penetrating radars. They should pick anything up.'

'How long before you have an answer?'

'One, two days, to cover the grounds. And then we'll check the house. There's a cellar. It looks clean, but we don't know for certain until we check it. Are you sure Aberman's dead?'

'It's a strong possibility. If he is, and he's here, then Helen Langdon's not looking so good.'

Isaac walked out of the front door of the house and walked around to the next-door neighbour. 'Mrs Hawthorne, you've been informed?'

'Is Mr Aberman buried there?'

'We've not been able to find him. The woman who used to come here, we believe her name was Helen Langdon.'

'Is she dead?'

'If it's confirmed she was the woman you spoke to, then yes?'

'Such a lovely woman. She gave me a vase for my house once. She said it came from her house.'

'Do you still have it?'

'It was too nice to use. It's still in the paper she wrapped it in.'

'Can we check it?'

'If you like.'

Isaac made a phone call. Grant Meston, Windsor's deputy, came over.

'Mrs Hawthorne has a vase in her house. The lady who used to check on Aberman's house gave it to her. There may be fingerprints.'

'I'll check it out now. It shouldn't take long.'

Isaac left Meston with the old lady and returned to the back of Aberman's house. A grid pattern had been laid out in the garden, and the two machines were going up and down at a slow pace. 'We can't hurry this,' Windsor said. 'It's been a few years, the ground's bound to have compacted.'

'Are you certain with the machines?'

'If there's a body, we'll find it. Grant said you may have a lead next door.'

'Fingerprints on a vase. If they're Helen Langdon's, then it's a further tie-in to the Dixey Club and Barry Knox.'

'Nasty piece of work, is he?'

'He's not someone you'd want to invite around your house. Denied everything, of course.'

'Don't they always.'

'The man's gone from pimping to running a strip club, so he's suspect to start with, and his bodyguard, he's the violent type. The sort of person who could kill Aberman.'

From the far end of the garden, one of the CSIs raised his hand. 'Over here,' he shouted.

'A result?' Isaac said.

'Don't get too excited. It could be a cat or a dog buried there. Whatever it is, it'll take most of the day to confirm.'

Grant Meston reappeared. 'Perfect prints,' he said.

'Whose?'

'Helen Langdon.'

Isaac phoned Larry and Wendy. 'It's confirmed. Helen Langdon was the mysterious woman at Aberman's house.'

'What next?' Wendy asked.

'We'll meet later tonight. The CSIs have found something in the garden.'

'Aberman?'

'Unknown. They're erecting a crime scene tent. From here on in, it's down to being on the ground and slowly sifting through the soil.'

A voice came from another part of the garden. 'Over here.'

'It's going to be a busy day,' Windsor said.

'Okay, call me when you have something,' Isaac said.

***

Isaac could see no advantage in staying around Aberman's house, and with a disciplinary hearing pending, he had to prepare his defence. Helen Langdon seemed the reason for the double killing at the hotel in Bayswater, but the waters were becoming muddied. It was now known that she had been involved in a relationship with Ben Aberman, the previous owner of the Dixey Club.

Larry was checking on the Adamants, trying to understand why and how Helen had married the father, whether the man's death had been as a result of his madness or whether he had been murdered.

Larry found the youngest child, Howard, at his place of work, the family home. 'How much money can you make doing this?' Larry asked, as Adamant sat in front of his monitor.

'It depends. Some weeks, a few thousand, others as much as fifty or sixty.'

'Serious money.'

'Hard work, long hours.'

'That's what I've got,' Larry said.

The man opposite continued working, although he was communicative. 'I've got to finish this today,' he said. 'Have you found out who killed Helen?'

'Not yet. She seems to have led a varied life.'

'What do you mean?'

'Before she met your father, she was performing in a club.'

'We know that. Dixey's. It's a dive.'

'You've been there?'

'Once or twice with some friends.'

'When Helen was performing?'

'Not then. They still had her picture outside, although I can understand why.'

'Why's that?'

'You've been?'

'Twice.'

'They're not much, the ones up on that stage. Helen, she must have been the star performer.'

'She was.'

'I can't imagine her with the men, the same as the others.'

'She wasn't, although she played along.'

'How do you know?'

'Some of my friends, they'd seen her there, but I never did.'

'You fancied her?' Larry said.

'Who wouldn't? She was more my age than my father's, but he had the money.'

'Apparently, the money wasn't that important to her.'

'What do you reckon? You're the policeman.'

'Money's always important, so's love. Helen seemed to prefer older men, no doubt they treated her better.'

'More likely to forgive and forget, and she flattered their egos. I would have taken her in an instant, but she'd seen through me.'

'What do you mean?'

'I was in my early twenties. I was into anything in a skirt.'

'It wouldn't have been serious with you, just another woman.'

'Maybe, maybe not, but I wasn't into settling down. Helen, if she wanted security and a decent man, that wasn't me, not back then.'

'And now?'

'I've grown up, money in the bank. Sometimes the stress of my work gets to me, and the idea of hitting the clubs, chatting up a woman doesn't appeal anymore. It's a shame about Helen. If she was in that room with James Holden, there was a reason; maybe it was love, but whatever it was, she's blameless.'

'Why so much devotion to the woman from everyone we've met? And we've been to Dixey's, we've spoken to your family, to Holden's family. What is it?'

'I don't know. Are you suspicious?'

'Nobody's that good. Everyone's got something they'd rather hide, skeletons best left hidden.'

'But you know her skeletons. She performed in that club, danced naked, took money from depraved onlookers.'

'Depraved?'

'You've been. What do you think?'

'You're right, I suppose.'

'It's the permissive society. If you want some titillation, to get laid, you just need to go out of a Saturday night, any pub, and there are plenty of females waiting for a man.'

'Is that what you do?'

'I've one or two women I can phone up. I'm doing alright for myself,' Howard Adamant said.

Larry could only agree with the man as he left the house. Outside, a Porsche, and the chance of a few women at the weekend. He remembered back to when he had been Adamant's age, a lowly police constable, a fifteen-year-old car. His chances had not been so good, but he had managed. His wife had been a Saturday night pickup, and they were still together after many years.

He envied the young man his good fortune but did not want it for himself. If he could just make it to detective chief inspector, he'd be satisfied.

Chapter 13

'You'd better get back to Aberman's house,' Gordon Windsor said on the phone.

'What is it?' Isaac said.

'We've found human remains.'

'Aberman?'

'It needs Forensics and Pathology to confirm. I'd say it was male judging by the clothes, but apart from that, I'd only be guessing.'

'I'll take your guess.'

'It's been here for five to ten years, maybe longer. There's no chance of facial recognition. Does the man have a relative we can use for DNA?'

'We've not looked.'

Isaac ended the call and phoned Larry. 'I've got Bridget and Wendy in the office. I need you out at Aberman's as soon as possible. Wendy and I will meet you there.'

'What's up?'

'A body. We're assuming Aberman's. Bridget, check if Ben Aberman has a close relative. Also, dental records.'

Larry was at Aberman's house within forty minutes, Wendy and Isaac not far behind. In the driveway was the next-door neighbour. 'Is it Mr Aberman? she asked.

'We've no idea yet. We'll come and talk to you later.'

'Such a nice man. Whatever next?'

'You didn't know of the man's history?'

'I told you before. He was in the entertainment business. He used to have all these attractive people down for the weekend.'

Isaac didn't feel it necessary to tell the woman that the attractive people were probably criminals and ladies of the night.

The three police officers kitted themselves up in overalls, foot protectors, and gloves. They proceeded around to the back of the house. In the far corner of the garden were a crime scene tent and Gordon Windsor. 'There are another couple of places to check. We were lucky with this one.'

'Not so lucky for the man in the hole,' Wendy said.

'Any sign of how he died?' Isaac asked.

'Bullet in the head, the hole's clearly visible,' Windsor said.

'What was it wearing?'

'A shirt. A pair of trousers, no shoes. He's laid out straight.'

'Are you saying they gave him a proper burial.'

'No. Whoever put him in that hole wanted to make sure he'd not be discovered. It's a deep hole, at least four feet. Normally, someone would just scrape off the topsoil and bury him, but not with this one.'

'Eventually the body would have been discovered,' Larry said.

'Would it?' Windsor said. 'That's not an assumption I'd make. He's buried under a compost heap, next to a fast-growing bush, plenty of roots. In time the body would have decayed into the soil.'

'Why in this garden?' Isaac said. 'There must be better places to bury a body.'

'It depends where the man was murdered. We're going through the house now. Nothing yet, and after so many years, and especially if someone's attempted to clean up, we may not find much.'

'Check for Helen Langdon's prints in the house.'

'We know what we're doing.'

'It's not looking good for the woman,' Wendy said.

'We'll go and have a conversation with the lady next door,' Isaac said.

'It'll be best if I go alone. An old woman might feel intimidated by you two.'

'Very well, you deal with it. Larry and I, we'll stay here, see what else they discover.'

***

Wendy knew it was better for her to talk to the next-door neighbour, a softly spoken woman. In her house, not as grand as Aberman's but still impressive, Wendy took a seat in the kitchen. 'What can you tell me about Mr Aberman?'

'He was a good neighbour, although I only saw him on weekends. The woman who used to come here was always polite.'

'Are you shocked by what we've found in Mr Aberman's back garden?'

'I don't know what to think. I've lived here for a long time, and it's the first time anything like this has happened.'

'It takes time to digest. Mrs Hawthorne, Ben Aberman had a dubious background.'

'Not Mr Aberman?'

'Your Mr Aberman was involved with criminals. The woman who visited you, she used to perform in one of his clubs. She was Aberman's girlfriend.'

'I never saw her at any of the parties.'

'Tell me about these parties,' Wendy said.

'They were loud, and sometimes they went on late.'

'You didn't complain?'

'I liked them. Some of the others around here would phone the police, but I used to watch from an upstairs window.'

'Did Mr Aberman know?'

'I told him once. He thought it was hilarious, invited me over the next time they had one, but that never happened.'

'He disappeared?'

'I thought he'd gone overseas, and then his friend turns up and asks me to keep an eye on the place.'

'I need you to think back to the last time you saw Mr Aberman. Is that possible?'

'He arrived at the house with some other men. I waved to him, but he didn't see me.'

96

'Anything else? The car they arrived in, the other men?'

'The car, it was black. It looked expensive, but I don't know what it was. I remember it being there for a long time, overnight, but there was no noise.'

'Did anyone go out into the garden at the back? You've seen where the crime scene investigators are.'

'Two men were digging a hole. I thought it was strange, but then, I'd seen the parties.'

'These parties, risqué?'

'Oh, yes. I'm not a prude. Some of the others in the area are, but I wasn't worried if they ran around half-naked.'

'What were they doing?'

'I was young once. I could only envy them.'

'The sort of things you wouldn't want a child to see?'

'I'm the only one who can see over the fence. Mr Aberman had good privacy, but my room upstairs can see right over. Some of them at the party, well, later on, they're on the grass.'

'And?'

'You know.'

'Indulging in sexual intercourse?'

'We used to call it screwing, but I suppose you're the police. You have to use the official term, make it sound dirty.'

'We use your word, but I thought you'd be offended.'

'My husband and I, we were broadminded.'

Wendy looked at the old woman, a gentle and kind soul, who had her family photos lined up on a table in the sitting room, a woman who treasured her knick-knacks, a woman who was not offended by the behaviour next door.

'Tell me about the men digging?'

'There's not a lot I can tell you. It was dark, and I couldn't really see them.'

'Did they see you?'

'Not me. I was careful to stay hidden. I get up in that room, the lights off, and I peer through a gap in the curtains. The two men, one was taller than the other, they didn't say much, only stopped for a rest every fifteen minutes. I could see they both smoked.'

'After they finished digging the hole?'

'I fell asleep before then. It was boring.'

'Did you fall asleep when they had the parties.'

'Not then. I loved to watch.'

'Mrs Hawthorne, you're terrible. A woman your age,' Wendy said, although it was said with humour.

'The mind's willing, even if the body isn't.'

'You said the car left in the morning.'

'It wasn't there, but it could have left during the night.'

'Did you hear any noises, any names mentioned?'

'Nothing, and my hearing's fine.'

'No gunshot?'

'Nothing. Do you think the woman who came here knew there was a body in the garden?'

'We don't know.'

'You could ask her. She gave me a phone number.'

'She'll not answer,' Wendy said.

'Any reason why?'

'The woman you know has died. She's been murdered.'

'Such a nice person. What a shame.'

'A shame, as you say.'

***

With the recovered body from Aberman's back garden with Pathology, the Homicide team gathered at Challis Street. Isaac was about to go through what they had so far when his phone rang.

'Linda Holden. Can you come to my office?'

'Is it important?'

'Yes. I've found something,' the woman said as she ended the phone call.

'Larry, you better come with me,' Isaac said. 'Wendy, can you focus on finding any relatives of Ben Aberman. Bridget, whatever you can.'

'Aberman was divorced,' Bridget said. 'Wendy could try there first. I've got an address for the ex-wife, no idea what sort of reception she'll receive.'

'I can handle myself,' Wendy said.

'You know what we want. We'll go and see what Linda Holden has, and then we'll swing by the Dixey Club, see what Knox and Gus have to say for themselves.'

'You should take Aberman's neighbour. She'd love it,' Wendy said.

'More than me,' Isaac said.

The two police officers arrived at Linda Holden's office. The place was almost empty.

'We've had to let most of them go,' Linda said on their entering.

'Why's that?'

'We survive mainly on benefactors, some wealthy, some through donations on our website, but with all the negative publicity, we're not bringing in enough money. Another month and we'll close the door.'

'Your mother?' Larry asked.

'She's confused as to what's happened. The Daisy woman, what about her?'

'Your father met her on an occasional basis. Their relationship was purely commercial.'

'But not with Helen?'

'That's what we've always believed. Helen, whatever else she was, was not a common prostitute.'

'Our father was obsessed with her. He was even considering leaving our mother.'

'You have proof?'

'I found some letters from him to her. I don't know if he sent them, and if he did, then why are they in this office?'

'Why are you telling us?' Isaac said.

'I'm closing this place down. I don't want any loose ends.'

'I thought your father's work was important.'

'Have you turned on the television lately?'

'Your father's no longer seen as the beacon of morality.'

'That's why I'm showing you these letters. They may help to explain my father's behaviour, they may not.'

'Your brother?'

'He's still angry. Although I think he's over the worst of it. He had been in love with Helen.'

'He could have killed her and your father?'

'If my brother had seen these letters, he would have been angry enough to do something.'

The truth is always the best approach,' Isaac said.

Larry took one of the letters and glanced through it. 'Not unusual for a man as he's getting older, the need to relive his youth, but, as you say, it was more than love.'

'That's Helen, isn't it? She has this power over men.' Linda said.

'Have you ever heard of a Ben Aberman?' Isaac said.

'Should I?'

'It's before Helen's time in prison. The man goes back to when she was performing. He was the owner of the club.'

'What about him?'

'We found a body in the back garden of his house. It had a bullet wound in the head.'

'Do you suspect the same person killed my father and Helen?' Linda said.

'There's a few years between the deaths. Up until the last few weeks, Helen had been paying regular visits to the house,' Isaac said.

'Did anyone know Helen? Do you think she killed her husband?' Linda said.

'Our primary focus is her death, not who she may have killed. Adamant treated her well. Even his children and they were older than her, treated her with respect.'

'Then maybe my father had no chance.'

'Maybe,' Isaac said. John Holden concerned him, and his sister had been right. The letters which Isaac now had in his pocket could have tipped James Holden's son over the edge from insanely jealous to vengeful and violent.

Chapter 14

'Christine Aberman?' Wendy said at the door of a smart terrace house in Chelsea.

'If it's about Ben, it's been years since I've seen him.'

'Sergeant Wendy Gladstone, Challis Street Police Station. I've a few questions.'

'Come in. You'll have to mind the house, we've got the painters in.'

'We?' Wendy said.

'My husband and I.'

'You've remarried?'

'Two years ago. A good man, more than I can say of Ben. I've kept his surname, though.'

'What did you know about your husband's business?'

'He ran some clubs, downmarket, sleazy.'

'Did it concern you?'

'No, should it?'

'Have you been to the clubs?'

'Never. He wanted me to go, to see where he made his money, but watching vacuous women gyrating around on a stage does nothing for me.'

'When did you divorce your husband?'

'Ten, maybe eleven years. The marriage had slowly been going downhill, and then he was staying away of a night every week or so. I smelt a rat.'

'What did you do?'

'I confronted him. He admitted he'd been fooling around, and that was that: no drama, no hysterics, no accusing the other. We phoned up a solicitor friend of ours. He came over to the house, dealt with all the paperwork. This house was part of the settlement.'

'It's very nice.'

'I know it is, and now my new husband is here with me.'

'What does he do?'

'Bank manager. It's not very glamorous, and it doesn't pay much, but that's not the point, is it?'

'What do you mean?'

'He's reliable, he treats me well, and he doesn't cheat on me.'

'Did you ever meet a Helen or a Daisy?'

'I never met any of his women, and besides, what's this about?'

'Your husband's house in the country. We've found a body in the back garden.'

'And?'

'You don't seem concerned.'

'My husband mixed with some unsavoury characters. If there's a body at the house, I'd not be surprised. Is it Ben?'

'We'll need to conduct further tests.'

'What do you want from me?'

'Dental records, or somewhere we can obtain them. Also, DNA.'

'I can give you the name of a dentist he used to use.'

'A photo?'

'It's a few years old.'

***

The Dixey Club with the lights on and in the middle of the day was not the same as Isaac and Larry had seen it previously. It was still too early for the women to be on the premises, although the manager, Barry Knox, was, as was his heavy, Gus.

'What do you want?' Gus said.

'Knox here?' Isaac said.

'He's busy unless you've got a warrant.'

'I've got a police car outside. It wouldn't take much to get a few uniforms to haul you off to the police station, let you cool your heels for a few hours.'

'On what charge?'

'Letting minors in, selling drugs.'

'I've not done that.'

'If you haven't, then you're the only door manager in the area who hasn't. We could always give you a strip search, check out where you live.'

'Okay, you've made your point. I'll get Knox for you.'

'Bit tough there,' Larry said.

'We need to put the pressure on these two. Knox knows something, and Gus, he's the guy who does the dirty work.'

After a few minutes, long enough for Isaac and Larry to look around the place, Barry Knox emerged. 'I've got a busy workload. Is this important?'

'The parties at Aberman's, did you ever attend?'

'What did I tell you last time?'

'Last time, you were playing us for suckers. We can either talk here or down at Challis Street. Which do you prefer?'

'We've done nothing wrong. We have all the licences in place.'

'What about the bed at the back? Is it licensed? What do you do with the video of the men with your women on the bed? Share it amongst your friends, indulge in a little blackmail?'

'The camera is for security. The bed is for first aid. We've been through this before. If you're trying to wind me up, you're wasting your time.'

'I could have you for half a dozen violations. What I want to know is why you and Gus were in Aberman's garden digging a hole late at night.'

'Are you serious? I'd been to his parties a few times, but it wasn't for gardening.'

'Cocaine, women, alcohol?'

'Why not? Aberman may have had his faults, but the man knew how to live, and he used to get some classy women there.'

'And the women were available?'

'That's why they were there.'

'Our crime scene investigation team have found a body buried in Aberman's garden. We also know two men dug the grave. One was short, looked like a weasel. The other one was tall, heavily-built, similar to a wrestler. Sound familiar?'

'You can't go insulting me like that,' Knox said.

'I can and I will until you start talking. Helen, was she ever at one of those parties?'

'I saw her there once, but she didn't take part. I told you before, she was strictly in the club as eye candy. She'd get the money from the men, and then Daisy and the other women would go in for the kill. Helen, she was Aberman's woman, and if anyone touched her, he'd have Gus take him out the back door.'

'A severe beating?'

'They'd not come back here again,' Gus said.

'Let's come back to what we were talking about,' Larry said. 'Ben Aberman has these parties. They're wild, and there's plenty of wrongdoing, but we're not interested in any of that. We're interested in why a body is buried in his garden. Now, the question once again. Did you two bury the man?'

'It wasn't us.'

'But you know who it was.'

'Gus,' Knox looked over at the heavy, 'it's up to you. What do you reckon?'

'I'm not going to jail for something I didn't do.'

'Do you want to tell us down at Challis Street or are you going to give us a statement here?'

'Okay, Cook,' Knox said. 'Here's what we know. Ben Aberman, he's a good operator, making good money, but he flies close to the wind, takes a few chances. He's keen to open two more clubs, but he needs money, and you've seen his house. Not the sort of place that a few clubs such as Dixey's will get you. The man borrows to maintain his expansion plans, his lifestyle. His parties are notorious, and he foots the bill, and the whores don't come cheap. He's over-extended, the lenders are calling in the money. Aberman's panicking, borrowing here and there, wherever he can. Eventually, he runs out of time, and the lenders come in here and take him.'

'Gus?' Isaac said.

'I'm only the hired help. The people who came here scared me. They were really mean. I act tough, but I'm not about to kill anyone.'

'Carry on, Knox.'

'I'm brought in as the replacement manager of this club, plenty of money, some bonuses.'

'Bonuses?'

'One or other of the women.'

'Helen?'

'She was promised, but two days later, she's out of here. Daisy's left, the poor substitute.'

'After Aberman left, what happened?'

'Not a lot. I was told Aberman had signed over the clubs, but for some reason, the house stayed in his name. That's the honest truth. Whatever happened, we don't know.'

'But you heard rumours?'

'There's always rumours, but me and Gus, we didn't give much credence to them.'

'What were they?'

'Helen had negotiated on Aberman's behalf, and for whatever reason, they agreed to the deal. And then two days later, Helen left the club. The word is that he's gone overseas, but I can't buy that. For one thing, the man's got a house and a lifestyle. And where overseas? That would need money, and Aberman, even if he was nothing else, was an Englishman. He had no connections overseas we knew of.'

'Is this just you two, or are there others who doubt the story?'

'We live on the edge, you know that, DCI. People come, people go. We don't have the luxury of asking too many questions, otherwise...'

'You disappear.'

'Aberman's not around, the club's still open. That's all we know.'

'You weren't surprised about Aberman's garden.'

'One night, a couple of years back, one of the lender's heavies is in here. He's had a few to drink. We know we need to look after him, so we bring him into the office. He wants to drink. We join in. He starts drifting in and out of consciousness. He starts talking, tells us about Aberman.'

'What did he say?'

'We're just making conversation, not trying to pry.'

'And?'

'The heavy, he's an ugly man, goes by the name of Pete. He says Aberman's pushing up daisies.'

'He's dead.'

'That's what we thought he meant, and he said afterwards it wasn't daisies, it was a bush of some description. He didn't say what type, probably didn't know.'

'Did you think it was Aberman's garden?'

'Only when you mentioned the body. Anyway, the man fell asleep, and the next morning, when he woke up, he didn't remember the night before. What was on top of the body?'

'A bush,' Isaac said.

'We've been honest with you two,' Knox said. 'Now, give us a break and don't ask us to repeat what we've just told you in a court of law.'

***

Graham Picket, the pathologist, a taciturn man, never appreciated having Isaac in his office, and now he had the full ensemble: Isaac, Larry, Wendy, and Gordon Windsor.

'What is it with you, DCI?' Picket said. 'I have the body for two hours, and you're bashing my door down for an answer. Your sergeant has brought me the dental records of a Ben Aberman.'

'Confirmed?' Isaac asked.

'I'll need longer to conduct a full autopsy, but the body, what's left of it, and the dental records match. If you go away, then I'm willing to state that the body in my care is that of Ben Aberman.'

'Thank you. A full report as soon as possible,' Isaac said.

With the confirmation the team had expected, the investigation had taken a different direction. Initially, it had been about a man and a woman naked and dead in a hotel. Then there was a prostitute, a former friend of the dead woman, who had died, and now a club owner, which indicated that organised crime was involved.

'It's not over,' Isaac said. Back in the office at Challis Street, the team were focussing on the situation. They were all fired up, ready to discuss the case and to get back out on the road, when the booming voice of their superintendent interrupted them.

'They're piling up again, DCI,' Seth Caddick said.

'It's under control,' Isaac said.

'You must be joking. Maybe I should come down here and give you a hand.'

'If you do, sir, I'll register a complaint.'

'Suit yourself. Remember the disciplinary hearing's next week.'

'I've not forgotten,' Isaac said.

And with that, the obnoxious Caddick left.

'He's baiting you, sir,' Wendy said.

'And doing a good job,' Isaac replied. 'Ignore the man and ignore what could happen. We need to focus on what we have. Larry, an update from you.'

'So far, our focus has been on Helen Langdon, not James Holden.'

'Is there a point?'

'Purely conjecture. Helen Langdon, the sinner redeemed, is looking increasingly suspect. And why Daisy? The woman left the club a long time ago, and she was only murdered after Helen. And what is this control that Helen has over Aberman's murderer?'

'She must have known he was buried in the garden,' Wendy said.

'A logical deduction. And how does she pull this off, this subterfuge? She came from an average family, average education, and, apart from her looks, she seems to be able to control whoever.'

'Men with their tongues hanging out,' Bridget said.

'Not so flippant as it sounds,' Isaac said. 'She's able to control men by her sexuality, but she doesn't give in. Apart from Aberman, we've found no other behaviour unbecoming of the woman. Are we sure that Helen and Aberman were sleeping together?'

'That's what we've been told,' Wendy said.

'But no proof. We know she married Adamant, and that was consummated, and there's a clear indication she had had sex with Holden, but no proof with Aberman. And if the man's killed, did she know, did she agree? She has his house, it's empty, and she could have moved in, but she didn't. Why not? All the bills have been paid, and she even had a debit card for the incidentals.'

'What about the solicitor who was looking after it for Aberman? He must have some correspondence with whoever's paying the money. If it's not Aberman, then who and why?'

'We're ruffling the feathers of some serious criminal figures,' Larry said.

'How do we get to them?'

'Knox mentioned Ugly Pete.'

'How do we find him?'

'I'll use my contacts,' Larry said.

'Fine, you follow up on him. Wendy, see what you can find out about Aberman and Helen. See if anyone is certain of their relationship, or whether it's just smoke and mirrors, and if it is, why? Bridget, do some research into Aberman's solicitor.'

Chapter 15

Nicholas Slater, the senior partner at the legal firm that Aberman had used, was not in a good mood when Isaac and Wendy entered his premises. 'I'm severely embarrassed,' he said.

'Your client does not appear to be Ben Aberman, does it?'

'I have carried out my duties meticulously.'

'Let's go back to when you took over the responsibility for the Aberman house,' Isaac said.

'Mr Aberman has entrusted me with his legal work for many years.'

'You've met him?'

'A long time ago. I knew his wife as well. I only visited his clubs the one time when there was a dispute over an alcohol licence.'

'Mr Slater, there are serious concerns regarding your propriety. When you visited the club, was Helen Langdon on the stage?'

'Aberman introduced me to a woman once. It was probably her.'

'How can you be unsure? The woman's picture has been in the newspapers, on the television.'

'Okay, it was Helen.'

Slater phoned for his receptionist to bring in refreshments. After the tea had been delivered, Slater spoke. 'Ben Aberman was a friend. We had known each other for many years, and I dealt with all his legal work. In the last couple of years, before he disappeared, he had become more erratic.'

'Any reason why?'

'Aberman was interested in expanding. He had split from his wife, a calming influence, and he was enjoying the freedom.'

'The women in the club?' Wendy said.

'Yes. Before that, he had regarded the clubs as places to make money, but there he is, early fifties, recently separated, and in a harem.'

'Helen Langdon?'

'Ben, he wants to make his mark. He makes contact with some people who'll help him out. I advised him against it, but he wasn't listening.'

'Can you prove your objection?'

'It's on file. Ben agreed to take the money from these people. I wasn't involved.'

'Did you see the paperwork?'

'There wasn't any. He was dealing with gangsters. They lent the money, you paid them back with interest, or they'd come and take it with force.'

'Aberman's got the money. He's done his homework. Why then, does he get into financial trouble?'

'He had lined up the purchase of another club, paid money upfront, and then the deal collapsed. Ben was frantic. He's down fifty thousand pounds, the lenders are after him, and he can't pay.'

'How do you know this?'

'He asked me to get him out of trouble.'

'What did you do?'

'I advised bankruptcy as the final solution, or to just walk away from the clubs, but Ben, he wasn't listening.'

'Bankruptcy wouldn't have been an option. The people he was dealing with would have still wanted the money.'

'I've always suspected the premises Ben had been looking at belonged to those who had lent him the money. They forced him into trouble, knowing full well that Dixey and the other clubs were cash cows.'

'Cash cows?' Wendy said.

'It's a financial term,' Isaac said. 'The clubs have been set up, and they're making a profit. All the gangsters need to do is to maintain the business and cream off as much money as they can. Aberman did the hard work, they reap the rewards.'

Ben, he was a fool,' Slater said. 'He decided to take them on.'

'You know a lot about this.'

'Ben's a friend. I advised him to prepare to leave the country. He was still not listening, but at least he was willing to consider my suggestion.'

'And when he disappeared?'

'I assumed he'd left the country. I already had access to one of his accounts. Out of friendship, I looked after the house for him.'

'That still doesn't explain Helen Langdon or the house being empty.'

'Helen, she's Ben's woman. Two weeks after my last contact with him, she entered this office. She was upset.'

'Why are you telling us this now?' Isaac asked.

'The situation is dangerous. Finding his body will only open old wounds. You're becoming involved in something dangerous. I hope you're prepared.'

'Are you?'

'I'm not sure I can be.'

'Continue,' Isaac said.

'The woman was not sure what to do. She told me this story about Ben, and how he'd got himself out of trouble by signing over the clubs, and she was going to look after the house for him."

'The money on her debit card?'

'That's covered. I asked her where Aberman is. She told me it would be best if I don't ask. Only that Ben's fine, and he'll be back one day.'

'Were you suspicious?'

'Ben always had a sense of the dramatic. After one year, more or less, the relationship with Helen is working fine. The house is empty, the woman is paying regular visits, and there's nothing more for me to do. I've other clients, and I gave little thought to Aberman.'

'Until?' Isaac said.

'Why do you say that?' Slater said.

'There's always an "until". You wouldn't be opening up to us unless there was a reason. You told us you didn't know Helen Langdon before, that you'd never met her.'

'Occasionally, Helen would phone me up.'

'Why?'

'She wanted to let me know that she was still around, and any attempt by me to enter the house would be met with retribution.'

'She knew what was in the house,' Wendy said.

'If she knew, then you did,' Isaac said to Slater.

'I did not. It was an unusual request, but I complied.'

'But the man was a friend who walked on the wild side. You must have been suspicious.'

'I was.'

'What did you do?'

'Several weeks ago, I was near to the house. I had a key in my pocket. It was an overcast day, and there was no one in the street. I took the opportunity to look around the house.'

'What did you find?'

'Nothing. It was not in good condition, and there was dust everywhere. I stayed about ten minutes and left.'

'No one saw you?'

'The old lady next door saw me leaving.'

'Did she talk to you?'

'No. I was too far away, but Mrs Hawthorne, she knew who I was. Before her husband died, I used to do some legal work for him.'

'Then what happened?'

'Nothing for a few days, and then Helen phoned me. She's angry, telling me I'd violated her trust, and our relationship would be severed forthwith.'

'What did you say?'

'Nothing. She hung up, and that was the last time I heard from her.'

'And when she ended up dead with James Holden?'

'I recognised her, knew her death was probably related to Ben Aberman. I was scared, not sure what to do.'

'Why was she killed?'

'She must have known that Ben Aberman was dead. But in all the years, she never dropped her guard.'

'What about the four years she was in jail?'

'I still received email correspondence.'

'Not from jail you wouldn't. Slater, you know more than you're telling us,' Isaac said. 'Unless you start giving us the truth, we'll be suspicious of you. You're too close to the action, maybe you killed Aberman. Maybe you're involved with these gangsters.'

'I'm innocent, believe me, but those that killed Aberman, they're dangerous. If they know I've been talking to...'

'They'll have you killed?'

'Yes. Even now, they're watching me.'

'Why would they be watching you? Apart from the one visit to the house, you've acted correctly.'

'I don't know why, and that's what frightens me. Helen, she could tough it out, but not me.'

'We've been told of a heavy who goes by the name of Pete. Any ideas?'

'I received a phone call,' Slater said.

'When?'

'Two days ago.'

'What did the person say?'

'I don't know who he was, only that he told me to be careful in what I said to you. I told him I knew nothing, but he didn't believe me.'

'Neither do we,' Larry said. 'You went into the house, you were curious, suspected something. I put it to you, Mr Slater, that you've always known Aberman to be dead and buried in that garden. Were you one of those at the house the night he died? Was it you who cleaned the house afterwards? And who was it who dug the hole in the garden? And who are the people who threatened the man and let Helen have the house, and why?'

'Helen, she was two-timing Aberman.'

'With who?'

There was a sound of shattering glass, a spray of blood, and Slater collapsed forward on his desk.

'He's been shot!' Isaac said. Both police officers moved from where they were and took shelter to one side of the window. Slater's receptionist opened the door on hearing the noise – another shot, and she collapsed to the ground.

Larry dropped to the floor and crawled over to where she was. He gently lifted her head. 'She's dead,' he said.

Isaac was on the phone, calling for backup. Wendy was on the way, as were Gordon Windsor and Caddick. The situation was dangerous. A quick glance by Isaac had shown a rooftop on the other side of the road. He couldn't see anyone there.

A phone call. Isaac answered. 'Specialist Firearms Command here. What's the situation?'

'Two dead. We'll try and move out of the line of sight.'

'Fifteen minutes, stay alive.'

'Slater knew the full story,' Larry said from his position on the ground next to the dead woman. 'She opened the door at the wrong time.'

Forty minutes later, the all-clear. 'No one up there,' the leader of the specialist firearms team said. 'A difficult shot, not sure I could have made it.'

Inside Slater's office were a team of medics, not that they could do much. Slater had been shot in the back of the head, his receptionist in the front.

'Nasty,' Caddick said as he entered the crime scene.

'Slater was about to tell us who had killed Aberman.'

'Out of here, everyone,' Gordon Windsor said. 'Isaac, you've got a right mess here. We'll need time on this one.'

Outside the building there was an ambulance; a medic checked out Isaac and Larry. Apart from shock and their clothes being covered in blood and shattered glass, they were declared fit.

'What's happened here?' Caddick asked.

'The man was covering for Aberman's murderers. He was about to give us a name.'

'The woman?'

'We think she was innocent. She's only worked for Slater
for a few months.'

'Where to from here?'

'Apart from a shower and a change, we've another
possibility.'

'Not for me to comment under the circumstances,'
Caddick said, 'other than to say we're all pleased that you both are
alive.'

'Thank you, sir,' Isaac said.

Caddick left, Wendy came over. 'We're dealing with
dangerous people,' she said.

'Larry and I need two hours. We'll meet in the office, go
over what we've got. Windsor can keep us updated, although we
were there, we know what happened.'

'We need a name,' Larry said.

'Whoever they are, they're watching.'

'But why Aberman's garden? If they had killed him
somewhere else, even thrown him overboard out at sea, we
wouldn't be investigating his murder.'

'More questions,' Wendy said. 'I'll stay here for now, and
we'll meet in two hours.'

Chapter 16

Larry's wife freaked out when he returned home. 'Not again. It's too dangerous,' she said. He tried to offer an explanation, but she wasn't listening. Isaac had no such person to complain. He was still on his own. The romance with the woman he had met in Brighton, a one-hour thirty minutes' drive to the south of London, had bloomed for a while, but then it had cooled down within a couple of months.

As he stood under the shower, lathering soap over and over again to remove the blood, the scent of death, he wondered if it was normal that the death of a solicitor and his young receptionist did not affect him.

He left the shower, dried himself, and put on a clean set of clothes. He put his old clothes in a large evidence bag, rather than dropping them off at the dry cleaner's. Caddick would have to sign expenses for their cost.

Two hours after leaving the solicitor's office, the team assembled at Challis Street. Bridget, as usual, was concerned and fussing. 'It must have been terrible,' she said.

'I could do with a pizza,' Isaac said.

'I'll order one,' Bridget said.

'Make that two.' Larry added his order.

'Three,' Wendy said.

Isaac could see Larry was suffering delayed shock. He made a phone call to the first aid officer in the building. She came down, gave Larry a tranquilliser and told him to take it easy, to go home and rest.

Larry thanked her, did not respond to her suggestion.

'You'd better not drive,' Isaac said.

Chief Superintendent Goddard phoned. 'I've requested a new date for your disciplinary hearing,' he said. 'With the recent developments, they've agreed. Also, Wendy Gladstone's medical, that's on hold.'

'Caddick?' Isaac said.

'Forget about him for now. You and Larry could have been shot. He'll keep out of your way for now, or if he's smart enough, he will.'

'Caddick and smart? Oxymoron, sir.'

'He's struggling to get his budget approved. Questions are being asked as to his effectiveness. There's an internal audit of all the senior officers. He's one of them.'

'Did Davies put that forward?'

'A government watchdog has made the recommendations. Davies will play it smart and put his full weight behind it.'

'Lord Shaw, DCS Goddard?'

'Don't go fishing, Isaac. Just be thankful that someone's still got the gumption to stand up and be counted.'

'How's Davies's position?'

'Don't expect him to depart soon. Worry about solving the current murders and try to make sure no one else dies.'

'We'll try our best, sir.'

Goddard ended the phone call. Isaac turned to the team. 'Wendy, your medical's been put on hold. Also, my disciplinary is off for now.'

'Caddick?' Larry said.

'He's got his own problems.'

'I'll go and see Mrs Hawthorne again,' Wendy said.

'Slater said he knew her, and she had seen him the day he visited Aberman's house. Mrs Hawthorne may well have enjoyed the spectacle of the parties, but she's nosey. Aberman was tortured, there must have been some noise.'

'I'll check out Slater's other clients,' Bridget said.

'Larry and I will revisit the Dixey Club,' Isaac said. 'Knox and Gus will be nervous now. If Slater can be killed, so can they, and they know who the villains are.'

***

Barry Knox was not pleased to see Isaac and Larry. It was late in the day when they arrived at the club. On the stage were two women, one upside down on the pole, the other teasing the patrons in the front row, tempting them to part with their money.

'You're here about Slater?' Knox said as Isaac and Larry entered his office. On the screens in one corner were the women out front, the audience, and the bed at the back of the establishment.

'Are you still looking at that bed?' Isaac said.

'First aid requires constant vigilance.'

'Did you know Slater?'

'He used to come along to Aberman's parties. Couldn't get enough of what was on offer.'

'What else can you tell us about him?'

'Not a lot. I never knew he was a solicitor until I saw a photo of him on the television.'

'We were there when he was shot,' Larry said.

'So much for the protection of the law,' Knox said. 'Don't bother offering me protection if I turn Queen's evidence.'

'Are you considering it?'

'I've nothing to tell you. I'm clean.'

'Twenty-four hours down at the police station may do you some good.'

'You can't hold me. I've done nothing wrong.'

'In this club? I'm sure if the vice squad come through here, they'll find something.'

'Okay, what do you want?'

'The truth.'

'Aberman, he was borrowing money.'

'We know this. And then he was in trouble.'

'That's it.'

'Who brought you in here to run this club?'

'The new owners.'

'Who are they?'

'I don't know.'

'What do you mean?'

'It's the honest truth. Apart from Ugly Pete, the heavy I told you about before, I've met no one. Our communication is by email and messaging.'

'An unusual relationship.'

'It suits me. I'm left to run the club, give them an agreed percentage of the takings, and I keep the rest after expenses.'

'Good money for you?'

'It's good. The women aren't complaining either. I expect the best, I pay the best.'

'They weren't bad-looking, the two out front,' Larry said.

'They're not. I've brought in some new women.'

'Slater was shot just as he was about to give us names,' Isaac said. 'Names you know. There's no window here, so nobody's going to take you out. It's either here or Challis Street.'

'These people don't mess around. If I tell you any more, I'm dead.'

'And if you don't, you're in jail.'

'Okay, Slater's death has got us all jumpy. Gus, he's taken off, trying to get some distance. I told him he's wasting his time, but then, he's not very bright.'

'What are you going to tell us?'

'Ugly Pete frequents a pub in Kensington, the Finborough Arms.'

'What does he look like?'

'I told you before. He's ugly, like a mongrel dog. And don't ask me any more. I still value my life, worthless as it may be to you.'

Chapter 17

Isaac realised that the murder enquiry had taken a turn for the worse. Before they had been looking for the murderer of two people in a hotel room, one a moral crusader, the other a former prisoner. Since then, a prostitute had been murdered, as well as a solicitor and his receptionist. And now there was the complication of the discovery of another body, Ben Aberman.

Isaac met his former senior not far from Scotland Yard.

'Public Relations isn't all it's cracked up to be,' Richard Goddard confessed.

'Davies didn't put you there to enjoy it,' Isaac said. 'He wanted you out of the way. It looks as though he's succeeded.'

'His time's coming, but that's not why we're meeting, is it?'

'I need to run the case past you.'

'Caddick?'

'The man's a fool. His advice is worthless.'

'What have you got?'

'Helen Langdon, four years in prison for killing her husband, subsequently acquitted. James Holden, moral crusader, member of parliament. The two of them are found naked in a hotel room, a bullet in the head each. Another prostitute, Daisy, a former work colleague of Helen's when they were both stripping, also murdered. Daisy was also meeting with Holden for the purpose of prostitution. We've assumed that Helen did not know about this.'

'That's three.'

'We discover the body of Ben Aberman, the owner of the club where the two women had worked. He was also Helen's lover during that period. Aberman's house has been empty for a long time. Helen's had been looking after it, along with a solicitor who was paid by Aberman. We were with the solicitor when he was killed. His receptionist, young and new at the firm, walked in the door and was shot too.'

'What's the common thread?'

'Helen Langdon, but she's dead. We've been looking for a murderer amongst Helen's circle of acquaintances, but now we're dealing with organised crime.'

'Is there any possibility James Holden was the primary target, and the subsequent deaths have been an unfortunate consequence?' Goddard said.

'It was a consideration initially. Holden was critical of the amount of dubious material that could be downloaded from the internet. He was a vocal supporter of tightening censorship guidelines, applying restrictions.'

'Are you suggesting a rethink?'

'Not totally. The discovery of Aberman's body has brought in an added complication. The earlier murders were the work of an individual, the later murders, as well as Aberman's, have the hallmarks of a crime syndicate.'

'The crime syndicate is more immediate. They don't mess around, could even take you out if you get too close,' Goddard said.

'What can be done about Caddick? He's a liability to Homicide and the ongoing investigation.'

'Davies will play his hand at some stage. The man knows Caddick is not up to the task. His strategy now is to bring back those who are. He'll make the normal platitudes about staff rotation, multitasking, and so on, but we'll know what it is.'

'A stalling tactic?'

'Davies may outlast us all.'

'A dreadful thought,' Isaac said.

***

Nobody expected Gus, the Dixey Club's bouncer and doorman, to walk into Challis Street Police Station. It was nine in the evening, and the team in Homicide were wrapping up for the day.

For three days, Caddick had not been seen: a training course for senior police officers. Larry had offered a comment when he'd heard about Caddick and training. Isaac had told him to be careful what he said and to whom.

'I've come to give myself up,' Gus said as he sat in the interview room.

'Do you need legal representation?' Isaac asked.

'Not this time.'

'What are you confessing to?'

'I was there the night Aberman died.'

'We've no one who can identify you. Why are you here?'

'They killed Slater. They'll kill me.'

'Did you kill Aberman?'

'No.'

'Did you bury him?'

'Yes.'

'What crime did you commit?'

'I helped bury the body, didn't tell you the truth. I was at Ben Aberman's house that night. They were upstairs with Aberman, working him over, trying to get him to sign over the clubs.'

'And you were downstairs watching the television.'

'Something like that.'

'Gus, you may fool others, but you don't fool us. Roughing a man up is one thing, shooting him in the head is another.'

'It was more than roughing him up.'

'The full story. We'll be recording this,' Isaac said.

'As long as you protect me.'

'Your full name?'

'Guthrie Boswell.'

Once Gus had been cautioned and advised of his rights, Isaac addressed him.

'In your own words.'

'Ben wasn't a bad man. He'd been running Dixey's for a few years. He treated the women well, especially Helen.'

'Were they lovers?'

'Yes. Ben was an ambitious man, wanted to do more. He borrowed money, gets into trouble.'

'How do you know this?'

'I was in the club. I'm the dumb muscle man, that's what everyone thinks, but I watch and listen.'

'And check out Aberman's office when he's not there.'

'Maybe there's some of that.'

'The night of Aberman's disappearance, what can you tell us?' Larry said.

'It's late, two in the morning. Ben in his office totalling up the money. I'm out front closing up.'

'Anyone else in the building?'

'The women have all left. Daisy's gone off with one of the customers. Helen went home on her own.'

'Aberman's home?'

'He had a flat not far from the club. She'd probably gone there, but I can't be certain. There's a knock on the door, I open it, and a gun is shoved in my face.'

'What did you do?'

'What anyone would do. I let the gun in.'

'How many men?'

'Three, and they're all armed. They demand to see Ben. I take them to his office. We've had problems with men demanding protection money before.'

'What has happened in the past?'

'Ben pays those who come in, and then afterwards, he finds out who they are. After that, they never return. The three guns, they're in Ben's office. One of the men is after the money owing. Ben, a stubborn man, is refusing. In the end, the men come out of the office with Ben held firmly between two of them. One of the men points a gun at me.'

'Did he speak?'

'He said either I'm with them, or I'm dead on the spot. Now, I'm not too smart to figure out what's going on most of the time, but this time, I know.'

'You went with them.'

'I figured Ben needed help, although I couldn't do anything in the club.'

'Ben was a friend?'

'He treated me well. I wasn't about to have my head blown off for him, but I owed him something.'

'Did you drive to Aberman's house in Bray?'

'That's it. Slater's already there. He's got some papers he wants Ben to sign.'

'And Ben refuses?'

'That's Ben.'

'Slater, what does he say?'

'I'm not that close, and they've handcuffed me. What I can make out is that Slater's trying to explain the situation.'

'Aberman's still not signing?'

'No. They take Ben into another room and start working on him. I can hear them from where I am, but I can't do anything.'

'No one in the area heard them?'

'These men, they're professionals. Ben had a gag so he couldn't scream, and the men, they're not talking, just hitting. They tell me he's going to sign or else they'll kill me first, then him. I'm panicking.'

'What did you do?'

'They gave me the option. Either I help them, or I'm dead.'

'You chose to help.'

'Whatever happened, I figured that Ben would still be alive, so would I, if I helped.'

'You trusted these men?'

'What option did I have? Ben looks at me, I say sorry, but he either signs or we're dead.'

'Then what?'

'They offered him the chance once again to sign, but he refused. They kept hitting him, and then one of them started on him with a lighted cigarette. Ben was in agony. I pleaded with him to sign, but he won't. In the end, they hooked him up to a handheld generator. He signed then.'

'Did they release him after he signed?'

'No. I go into the other room to figure out what to do next. I wanted Ben and me out of there, but the men with Slater, they don't look to be the forgiving kind. One of them came up to me.'

'What did he say?'

'He told me again, that I'm either with them or I'm not. I'm dragged into the other room, and there's Ben, his head covered in blood. The gun must have had a silencer as I never heard any sound.'

'You're freaking out, you're next. What do you do?'

'I've no option.'

'You were one of those who buried Ben in the back garden?'

'I helped to dig the grave.'

'And who was the other man?'

'Pete, that's all I know.'

'Ugly Pete?'

'Don't say that to his face. He's an angry man. He was the one who shot Ben.'

***

'You've charged the man with accessory to murder, is that it?' Superintendent Caddick said on his return from the course.

'It won't be long,' Isaac said. 'We've a lead on the murderer.'

'It's Holden that Commissioner Davies is interested in, not the owner of a strip club.'

'Murder's equal in the eyes of the law, the penalty is the same.'

'You've been meeting with Goddard from what I hear.'

'Is there a problem?'

'Suit yourself, but I'm in charge of this place, not him.'

'He's a personal friend,' Isaac said.

'Soon to be out on his ear.'

'Is he?'

'Goddard, he's playing politics. One wins, another loses.'

'Are you, Superintendent Caddick, intending to be one of the winners?'

'That I am.'

'For myself, I intend to succeed by good policing.'

'That's the problem, Cook. You're an idealist. The world is not what you believe. You've seen into the gutter on enough occasions. You know that people such as yourself are doomed to lose.'

'That's your view, not mine.'

'Very well. How long before you bring in Holden's killer?'

'Soon.'

'We'll see. You're off the disciplinary for now after the shooting in the solicitor's office. Made yourself some sort of hero, but how did they know you were there and what was being said?'

Several minutes after Caddick had left, Larry came into Isaac's office. 'He's right,' he said.

'Caddick, I don't think so.'

'I'm not saying he came up with an original thought, but how did they know what we were talking about, and why shoot Slater when we're in his office? They could have done that anytime.'

'Ugly Pete, any success?'

'I've got a lead on him and an address. I've got men keeping a watch on his house. The moment he's spotted, we're going in.'

'The pub?'

'He's keeping away from there. If he killed Aberman, and he knows that Gus is in custody, he would realise we're looking for him.'

'How did you get the address?'

'Ugly Pete's not a popular man. He's known for his rough tactics, and there are a few who wouldn't mind seeing him off the street for a while.'

'More than a while if he killed Aberman. Could he be the sniper at Slater's?'

'It's not likely. The man's not fit, moves slowly, and he's not known for using a gun. He's more into fists.'

'According to Gus, he killed Aberman.'

'Gus is scared of what could happen to him, or is he trying to shift the blame?'

'Either. We'll need Ugly Pete in here to know the truth. And Helen Langdon? She's the tie-in between Aberman and Holden. How could so many people be so wrong about her?'

'Focus on Ugly Pete. He'll help to fill in the blanks.'

Chapter 18

Wendy Gladstone maintained her visits out to Mrs Hawthorne, Aberman's neighbour. The woman was forgetful and glad of the company. After her third visit, Wendy could recite the Hawthorne family history, of how her husband had made his money in the city, how Mr Aberman had moved in several years after her husband had died, and how the man had helped her when she needed it.

'We've found one of the men who dug the hole in Mr Aberman's garden,' Wendy said.

'There were two.'

'We've got a description and a name for the other one. Mr Slater, the solicitor, do you remember him?'

'Yes. My husband used him occasionally.'

'He was at the house the night that Mr Aberman died.'

'He may have been. It was dark that night, and there were no lights in the driveway.'

'We've also been told that he would attend the parties.'

'I can't remember seeing him there, but that's not surprising.'

'Why?'

'I can't see very well, really. I could tell if it was a man or a woman, but apart from that, it wasn't so easy.'

'We have reason to believe Mr Slater was involved in Mr Aberman's death.'

'My husband didn't like the man, but he thought he was competent.'

'On the night Mr Aberman died, you said you didn't hear any noise.'

'There was some noise, but it wasn't a party. There were no women there.'

'What sort of noise?'

'Voices, that's all.'

'We know that Aberman was shot in the house. Are you saying you didn't hear the shot?'

'I went to sleep early. No party, no fun.'

Wendy realised the woman could offer little more. She left and walked around to Aberman's house. In the driveway, a car. 'Mrs Aberman, this is a crime scene,' she said.

'I just wanted to see the place.'

Wendy found the woman's presence disturbing. 'We need to talk,' Wendy said.

'If you want. Here?'

'Not here. I suggest we go and sit in my car.'

Seated in the car, Wendy turned to the woman. She could see that the ex-Mrs Aberman was not comfortable with the situation. 'You knew your former husband owned this place?'

'He bought it before we separated. When we divorced, I kept the house in London, he kept this one.'

'Which one do you prefer?'

'I always preferred this one, but Ben liked to have his parties.'

'And this house was better?'

'Yes.'

'You knew about the parties while you were married?'

'They were tamer when I lived with him, and Ben, he behaved himself. He changed with time, became more of a risk-taker, and some of the people he associated with, well, they were disturbing.'

'Explain.'

'More criminal. Some of them were charming, especially the more important ones, but they'd arrive with extra men, men who'd sit outside in the car or lean against it. I think some of them carried guns.'

'Tell me about the parties when you were here.'

'Ben liked to entertain. I would go on about the cost, but he said it was good for business. Not that I understood how, but the man was a good provider, so I left him to it.'

'Women?'

'There'd be women, and yes, couples were pairing off, but it was nothing serious. And Ben stayed with me. Sure, there was too much alcohol, and some of the guests were into cocaine. I would have preferred a quiet night at home with a bottle of wine, but that wasn't to be. It was the parties that drove us apart.'

'Helen?'

'I'd heard the rumours about her, but I ignored them. I married Ben when we were both young, and he was always faithful. I knew about the clubs, can't say I approved, but Ben liked to live on the edge, and in time I accepted his unusual way of making an income.'

'The man changed?'

'Not for a long time.'

'The suspicious signs?'

'Lipstick on the collar, not kissing me on coming home, straight in the shower. The signs were there, but for a long time I ignored them. I just didn't want to believe them.'

'What convinced you?'

'I paid someone to check out the club. A private investigator. He visited the club, found my husband in a compromising position with one of the women. I know people expect the owner of a strip club to be nefarious, but Ben wasn't like that. We were a conventional married couple at home, but in the club, he was the sleazy manager of a sleazy club. Almost like play acting.'

'What happened when you found out about the other woman?'

'I confronted him. He admitted to his guilt, and that was that.'

'You must have seen him from time to time.'

'I did for a few months, and then, after that, rarely.'

'Did you know Nicholas Slater?'

'We used the man for the purchase of the house in Bray. I didn't like him very much.'

'He was shot.'

'I know.'

'And yet you come to this house knowing full well that whoever shot him could be watching this house.'

'In the event of Ben's death, this house belongs to me. It was in the divorce settlement.'

'Your husband disappears for years, and you were never suspicious?'

'What could I do? And besides, I had no need of the house. I was, am, comfortable with what I've got, and I don't have the searing ambition that Ben had, but now the house is here, and I'd like it back.'

'He was killed in the house.'

'I know, and probably I'll sell it.'

'Can you prove the house is yours?'

'Yes, I can. Slater and my solicitor drew up the agreement. I have a document at home signed by both parties.'

***

On the fourth day of staking out Ugly Pete's house, he appeared. By that time the two teams that had been rotating to watch the house were bored, and if it had not been for one of the men looking over towards the house at the last minute of their shift, they would have missed him.

Ugly Pete's house, 34 Victoria Street, Croydon, was not everyone's idea of a desirable residence. It was on the rougher side of the area and getting rougher. On the footpath outside, a broken chair had been dumped for the council to pick up. Inside the front gate were an old bicycle, a discarded child's toy.

Isaac and Larry drove over to the man's house, even though it was one o'clock in the morning. At the back of the house, two uniforms waited. Out front, an armed response team. The man inside was known to be dangerous and probably armed.

Sergeant Gaffney of the Specialist Firearms Command knocked on the door – no response. He hit it harder the second time. A window opened upstairs. 'What do you want?' a gruff voice said.

The light of a street lamp shone in the man's face. 'I can see why they call him ugly,' Larry said.

'Police,' Gaffney said.

'Can't a man have a good night's sleep?'

'If you open this door, we can resolve this in a few minutes.'

The head at the upstairs window pulled back. 'He's getting ready to make a run for it,' Isaac said.

Gaffney gave the instruction. 'This man is regarded as extremely dangerous.' With that, another officer took hold of a battering ram and slammed it into the front door. It opened with no difficulty. A man was coming down the stairs in a hurry. 'Police,' one of the officers shouted. A short scuffle, an attempt to draw a weapon, and then Ugly Pete was handcuffed and in the back of a marked police car.

'Where to?' the driver of the car asked.

'Challis Street Police Station. Put him in one of the holding cells for now,' Isaac said.

He and Larry entered Ugly Pete's house and looked around, careful not to disturb anything. Downstairs was spartan and not clean. Upstairs, only one of the rooms had a bed. It was dirty; the sheets had not been changed for some time.

'We need a weapon,' Larry said. 'I'll stay and check the place.'

'Do we need the crime scene examiners here?' Isaac said.

'Not yet. There's been no crime here except against good taste.'

***

'I've done nothing wrong,' Ugly Pete said. He was in an interview room. He had accepted legal aid. Wendy had one conviction against him, his lack of hygiene; the man stank of body odour and stale beer.

'Your full name,' Isaac said.

'Peter Foster.' Isaac could tell the man had not shaved or showered for several days. His face was marked, the result of childhood acne, his nose twisted to one side. He was also short, matching the description that Gus and Mrs Hawthorne had given.

Isaac was sure that Ugly Pete was Ben Aberman's killer, but he didn't look to be the sort of person to admit to anything. The only witnesses on that night were the old lady next door – and it had been dark, and her eyesight would not have been that good – and Gus, the Dixey Club's doorman.

'Mr Foster, you are aware of the Dixey Club?'

'Not me.'

Isaac leant over to the man's solicitor. 'I suggest you advise your client to answer questions when given. We know that Mr Foster frequents the area near to the club. A denial does not assist his case.'

'What case is this?' Ugly Pete said.

'You've been informed. The murder of Ben Aberman.'

'Who?'

'Mr Foster, we can confirm that you were at a house in the village of Bray when Ben Aberman was killed. We have two witnesses who will confirm that.'

'Was I? That's news to me.'

'Ben Aberman, the owner of the Dixey Club, was beaten and tortured in that house. He was then shot, a bullet in the head.'

'What's that to do with me?'

'We have a witness who will testify that you shot the man, and then you buried him in the garden of the house.'

'Not me. I've killed no one.'

'Are you going to continue to deny your knowledge of this house?'

'I've never been there.'

'Stupidity is not a defence,' Wendy said.

'If you've no proof, then why is my client here?' the legal aid said.

'Ben Aberman had a woman. She called herself Helen.'

'I don't know her either,' Foster said.

'She was a dancer at the club. She was recently shot in a hotel in Bayswater, together with a man. Also, she had a friend, Daisy, who was murdered.'

'Are you trying to pin all of them on me?' Ugly Pete said.

'Not all. You did not kill the two in the hotel, nor Daisy. Those killings required a person of stealth. You're not stealthy, more brute muscle. Another two murders, Aberman's solicitor and his receptionist. Yet again, you could not have done it. It would have required an agile man to be on the roof opposite their office.'

'You've got nothing on me,' Foster said.

'You're a man with a record. How many times have you been charged with assault, how many convictions?'

'I'm a violent man, but it doesn't make me a killer.'

'Mr Foster, you know who the men are who gave Aberman the money, the men who wanted it back. Aberman, we know, was not a person to be intimidated. That's why you went to work on him in Bray, why you killed him, and why you and Gus, the doorman at the Dixey Club, buried Aberman in the garden. Gus is going down for enough years as it is. He'll identify you as the killer if it reduces his sentence. And what about your fingerprints at the house?'

'I wore…'

'Gloves, is that what you were about to say?'

'My client is not in a position to continue this interview. I am requesting that this interview is reconvened at a later time when Mr Foster has had a chance to change his clothes and to have a shower.'

'I don't think Ben Aberman had such courtesy when he was being beaten and tortured by Mr Foster,' Isaac said.

'My client vigorously denies his involvement.'

'Mr Foster, we will be charging you with the murder of Ben Aberman. The person who buried the body with you will testify it was you who was the murderer.'

'I'm innocent.'

'The only way you can hope for some leniency is if you tell us who were the other men at Dixey's the night you took

134

Aberman. We know there were three. Who were the other two? And who or what is the organisation that Aberman signed the clubs over to? What is Helen Langdon's significance in this?'

'My client needs time to consider his position,' the legal aid said.

'Thirty minutes.' Isaac said.

Chapter 19

Isaac took the opportunity of a break in questioning Ugly Pete to phone Larry.

'I've found a weapon at Ugly Pete's house,' Larry said. 'It took me a while. I just followed the dust in the house, found a clean spot. It was there, under a floorboard.'

'Forensics, how long before they can give us a positive that it's the weapon that killed Ben Aberman?'

'It's fitted with a silencer. Not legal in the UK, but Ugly Pete wouldn't care. I'll take it to Forensics myself. We should have an answer today.'

'The man's playing tough. He doesn't want to admit to anything.'

'If he's convicted of Aberman's murder, he's not likely to see freedom for a long time.'

The interview reconvened. Isaac had more ammunition with which to get the reluctant man to talk.

'My client wishes to make a statement,' the legal aid said. Isaac thought he was too young to be a solicitor.

'When he's ready,' Isaac said.

'I, Peter Foster, did not kill Ben Aberman. I knew of the Dixey Club, having been there on a few occasions. At one time, I was hired to visit the club in the early hours of the morning with two others. I do not know their names. The purpose of the visit was to escort Mr Aberman to his house in Bray. There was a Mr Slater present. After we had delivered the man, I left.'

'Is that it?' Isaac said.

'That's all I've got to say,' Ugly Pete said.

'Your solicitor has not advised you well. Although in his defence he does not know of your history, nor of certain facts. Before we go any further, let me outline what we know,' Isaac said. 'We have found a weapon at your house. Hiding it under a floorboard was not enough to deter Detective Inspector Hill. It is fitted with a silencer and is almost certainly the weapon that killed Ben Aberman. We do have a bullet from where the murdered man was buried. Also, we have Guthrie Boswell's testimony that Mr Foster killed Aberman, and that he and Mr Foster buried the body in the garden.'

'I had to do it,' Foster said, leaping to his feet.

'Why?'

'If I hadn't shot him, they would have shot me.'

'That's not a defence,' Wendy said.

'I received this phone call. The man's insistent it's a pickup, a roughing up, make him sign a piece of paper. Nothing more, I swear it.'

'Your speciality?'

'That's what I do. Men such as Aberman get down in the dirt. They don't like it when they're called to account.'

'Why kill Aberman?'

'I don't know, but that's what I was told to do.'

'By who?'

'Slater.'

'And he's dead.'

'I only ever received text messages to be at a certain place at a certain time. The money's paid into my account.'

'You had the gun. You could have refused.'

'Not with the people Slater represented.'

'Which people?'

'People who stay hidden, people who would have me killed. That's the truth.'

'Who are they?'

'I don't know. You can keep me in here for as long as you like. I can't tell you any more.'

***

Linda Holden closed her father's morality campaign office the day after Ugly Pete was charged with the murder of Ben Aberman. One week later her brother, John, was dead.

'He'd been depressed for some time,' Linda said when Isaac met her at her family home.

'Your mother?'

'She's not been the same since our father died, almost reclusive.'

'Why was your brother depressed?'

'With John, you couldn't be sure. He'd attempted suicide before. This time he stepped in front of a train. He wanted to let us know that the guilt lies with us.'

'And does it?'

'My mother feels guilt, I don't. John was a weak person, always ready to blame his problems on others. Our father had no time for him.'

'Was it mutual?'

'They rarely spoke, and once Helen had made it clear she did not want his son, their relationship became worse.'

'I have to ask. Would John have been capable of murder?'

'He would have hated his father being in that room with Helen, but I still don't think he could have killed them.'

'Sisterly love protecting you from the truth?'

'It could be.'

'We have reason to believe that Helen Langdon was a fraud. The more we discover, the deeper we go, we find more negative aspects of the woman. In your time with her, did you ever sense anything unusual?'

'She was besotted by my father, that was clear, but if, as you say, she was a fraud, how much was genuine?'

'Why the hotel room?' Isaac said.

'Our father strayed occasionally, but why with Helen? And what about Gerald Adamant?'

'There's a new investigation into his death.'

'Is the verdict against Helen likely to be changed?'

'That's not our primary concern. We're focussed on who killed your father and Helen,' Isaac said. 'Regardless of what or

138

who she may have been, the two were shot in that room. We've focussed on Helen because she has a past, but it's always possible that the murderer was targeting your father, and if he was, then why, and why in a hotel room? It would have been easier to kill him elsewhere.'

'Maybe Helen being with him was the reason. Maybe they wanted to destroy his reputation by exposing him as a debaucher, not a paragon of virtue.'

'Outside of that room, his murder would have strengthened his moral campaign, but in that room, regardless of his dying, he becomes painted as the sinner.'

'And with Helen Langdon, the wife of Gerald Adamant, the man she killed.'

'Whoever killed him knew what they were doing,' Isaac said.

***

Isaac's conversation with Linda Holden had offered him a fresh approach to the first murder investigation. He was in his office at Challis Street. The team were there.

'James Holden's son has committed suicide. His father's morality campaign office has closed.' Isaac said.

'It's not surprising after he's caught in a hotel with a former stripper,' Wendy said.

'That's the issue, isn't it? The man's reputation destroyed in an instant.'

'Did the killer get a tip-off, two birds with one stone?'

'Daisy knew them both. Maybe she recognised them going into the hotel, told someone. And whoever killed the two lovers killed her to tie up loose ends.'

'Was your concierge on duty the time they were killed?'

'Yes.'

'We need him in here now.'

Larry left Challis Street and drove the short distance to the hotel. Inside, at reception was another person. The hotel still had the look of neglect, and a woman could be seen sneaking in with her man for the hour. 'Is the other concierge here?'

'The hotel fired him,' the new concierge said. Larry looked at the man: Slavic, poor English, unpleasant look.

'Do you know where he is?'

'He found a job around the corner. And what's it to you?'

'Challis Street Police Station. Detective Inspector Larry Hill, or didn't you see my ID card when I showed it to you?'

'I saw it. Serge, he's a friend of mine, that's all.'

'Why was he fired?'

'He was letting people into the hotel without paying.'

'You're doing the same from what I can see.'

'Serge, he asks too many questions.'

'What sort of questions?'

'The sort I don't ask.'

'Are you going to continue talking nonsense, or am I going to haul you down the police station?'

'People come in here, people go out. They pay their money, sign in the book. Apart from that, I don't care what they do, with whom, and how. That way, I keep my job and make a little extra on the side. But my friend, he's inquisitive, wants to see what they're up to, who's with who. The management finds out that he's been spying on people. They're not happy, he's sacked.'

'Are you still letting the prostitutes in?'

'As long as they pay.'

'The management, they get a percentage of what you take?'

'That's the agreement.'

'Did you know Daisy?'

'She used to come in here occasionally.'

'She was killed because she knew the two in room 346.'

'I wasn't here that night.'

'What about the room?'

'It's still closed. It's being repainted.'

'Take me up there,' Larry said.

'I can't. I've got to man the desk. I can give you a key.'

Larry took the key and walked up the stairs to the third floor. Outside the murder room, he paused. Down the hallway, the sound of a woman with her customer: she making the mandatory noises; he attempting to pretend it was love. It was clear the man was drunk. Larry opened the door to the murder room. In the middle of the barren room was the bed where the two had been shot. A trauma scene clean-up team had been through the room. There was no sign of what had happened, only a faint whiff of cleaning fluids. The carpet that had been on the floor had been removed, as had the mattress and the sheets. In the wardrobe, there was nothing, not even a wire coat hanger. Larry looked in the bathroom, yet again spotlessly clean. He imagined there'd be couples in the future, lying on the bed, making love, not knowing that once two others had died violently on it. Larry closed the door on his way out.

Downstairs, he gave the key to the concierge and left. No words were exchanged. It was not far to walk to where Serge, the previous concierge, was.

'I can't tell you any more,' he said. Larry could see the hotel was better than the previous one, and Serge had cleaned himself up.

'No ladies of the night?' Larry said.

'They're strict here.'

'No more peeping, no more taking money to turn a blind eye.'

The concierge did not respond to the bait. 'I've told you all I know. The last time I pointed out someone to the police, she ended up dead.'

'What is it you've not been telling us?'

'What do you want me to tell you? The room was on the third floor, I'm on the ground floor. Two people come in, they pay for a room. She's attractive, he's older.'

'You didn't think it suspicious?'

'We're a hotel. If they pay their money, don't steal the contents from the minibar, what is there to be suspicious about?'

'You were watching couples in their rooms.'

'Who said I did?'

'Don't deny it.'

'Sometimes, when it's quiet, I like to look around.'

'Small hole in the wall?'

'Yes.'

'You couldn't resist Helen Langdon. The woman was beautiful, not like the women who normally came in, not like Daisy.'

'The hotel was quiet. I sneak away for a few minutes. I had the key to the next room. There's a small hole in the wall behind a picture.'

'What did you see?'

'The two of them in bed.'

'Sleeping?'

'Screwing.'

'You're excited, enjoying the spectacle. Then what happens.'

'The bell on reception goes. I've got a remote that beeps. I leave them to it.'

'How much longer before they're dead?'

'According to your people, fifteen minutes, maybe thirty.'

'At the reception, what do you find?'

'Another woman with her customer.'

'You give them a key?'

'She's a regular. I know she'll fix up the money later, and besides, the man looks as if he's in need of her.'

'What do you mean?'

'He's pawing her, trying to kiss her.'

'Her reaction?'

'She's playing along. The man looks as if he's got money.'

'Who was the woman?'

'Daisy's flatmate.'

'Gwendoline?'

'That's her. She's been in the hotel more often than Daisy.'

'Why didn't you tell us this before?'

'Tell you what? You were looking for a man, not a prostitute.'

'And you didn't want us to find out about your snooping.'

'What are you going to do about it?'

'Nothing. We've got to find this woman. Does she stand on a street corner near here?'

'The same places as Daisy.'

Larry left the man and phoned Wendy. 'Meet me in Bayswater. We need to find Daisy's flatmate, Gwendoline. You know her better than me.'

***

Larry and Wendy drove around the area looking for the usual spots where the women congregated. Gwendoline was nowhere to be seen. Eventually, the two of them visited the brothels in the area. Around the back of Paddington Station, they found the prostitute. She was sitting on a leather sofa on the first floor of a brothel. On either side of her were two other women; one was South American, the other looked Asian.

'They're probably in this country illegally,' Wendy said.

'We're here for Gwendoline, not them.'

'What do you want?' Daisy's flatmate said.

'We've some questions for you.'

'I'm busy, come back later.'

'Later doesn't work for us,' Larry said. He could see the woman was agitated. She was wearing a dress so short that her underwear was visible. She was not wearing a bra.

'Five minutes, that's all I can give you.'

'We need you down at the police station. You can go like that or do you want to change?'

'I don't want any trouble in here,' the madam of the brothel said. Wendy saw a woman in her fifties, almost certainly an ex-prostitute. In the corner of her mouth a cigarette, its ash ready to fall on the floor.

'It's not as good as the hotel you used to use,' Wendy said to Gwendoline.

'It's safer here.'

143

'What do you mean?'

'Daisy, she was murdered, and then those two in that room at the hotel.'

'Did you use that room?'

'Sometimes.'

'Gwendoline, I don't want the police in here,' the madam said. 'Go with them, come back later.'

The prostitute picked up her coat and left with Larry and Wendy. She complained, although no one was listening. At Challis Street, she was placed in one of the interview rooms and given a cup of tea, as well as some biscuits. 'I'm hungry,' she said.

'Pizza?'

'Hawaiian.'

Twenty-five minutes later, with the woman fed, Larry and Wendy commenced the interview.

'You were in the hotel on the night of the murders in room 346.'

'A waste of time for me.'

'What do you mean?'

'I'm doing a favour for Daisy. She says the man pays well, and he'll see me right.'

'Why didn't she take him?'

'She wasn't feeling well, and the man phoned at the last minute.'

'You agreed?'

'Why not? I met him at the hotel, and we went up to the room.'

'Which room?'

'The one opposite the murders.'

'What happened?'

'He gave me a drink. I wake up three hours later.'

'Was the drink drugged?'

'I suppose so. Anyway, I've got a throbbing headache. I put on my clothes and leave the hotel, that bastard on the door wanting his money, as well.'

'Your customer, did he pay you?'

'No.'

'There's a murder in the room opposite. You're unconscious, the man you're with has disappeared. Doesn't that sound coincidental to you?'

'I don't get involved, the first rule for people like me. We don't ask for their life story, or whether life has treated them bad or good. We're not a confessional, either. It's sex and out of the door.'

'Did this man murder Helen Langdon and James Holden?' Larry asked.

'He could have killed me,' Gwendoline said.

'You were his way into the hotel. Did the concierge see you downstairs?'

'He did.'

'Describe this man?'

'What's to describe. I don't check them out, prefer to look away.'

'Regardless of whether you look or not, what can you tell us about him?'

'Average height, white. He spoke well.'

'Did he give a name?'

'Dennis, but that's probably not his name.'

'Why?'

'Most of them make up a fancy name. Somehow it helps them to deal with the guilt.'

'Is that why you're Gwendoline instead of Kate Bellamy?'

'The men want the strange names, I only want their money. There's no guilt from me. I'm a spaced-out junkie, nothing more, nothing less.'

'Let's come back to this man. Did you have sex with him?'

'No. He gave me the drink and then nothing.'

'Did you believe him to be the murderer?'

'I didn't think about it. He probably was, but I don't know. I was frightened.'

'Daisy, what did she say?'

'She said she was surprised. He had always been fine with her. A few days later, she's murdered in our flat.'

'It's probably the same man. Why did he leave you alone? You could identify him, the same as Daisy.'

'I couldn't. I told you, I don't study the men. With them, I'm an empty vessel. Mentally, I'm detached. If you ask me about the men from last night, I couldn't give you detailed descriptions.'

'Do you dislike your life?' Wendy asked.

'It's not my choice. I'm addicted, that's all. The men feed the habit, I forget.'

Chapter 20

Isaac sat with Violet Holden; she was subdued. Linda Holden sat close by.

'Mrs Holden, I'm sorry about your recent losses, but there are questions I must ask,' Isaac said.

'Please ask.'

'Mother's on sedatives,' Linda said.

'I'll take it easy. Please say if you have anything to add.'

'I will. The last few weeks have been difficult.'

'Mrs Holden, Linda, I want to update you on our enquiry. There are some concerns that you may be able to clarify.'

'We'll do what we can,' Linda said.

'We know of Helen's background, although it's still difficult to understand what was in her mind. All indications are that she and James Holden were killed because of her. She had probably known of the death of Ben Aberman, a former lover, and where he was buried. For whatever reason, she kept it secret. There's also her marriage to Gerald Adamant. Every person we've spoken to saw it as a love match.'

'You're not sure now,' Violet Holden said.

'It was everyone's faith in Helen that ultimately led to her reduced sentence after she killed Adamant with a hammer.'

'If people had not believed in her?'

'Without the character witnesses, she may have been found guilty of first-degree murder. That's conjecture on my part. Is it possible that Mr Holden was the intended target? He must have upset a few people over the years.'

'He was introducing a bill into parliament that would have given sweeping powers to block websites that showed dubious content.'

'Those safeguards are in place now,' Isaac said.

'They're subject to intervention, debate. He wanted to set up a team of people whose decisions would be final. They could switch off a site on picking up an offensive word, a suggestive image.'

'Can't they do that now?'

'They can, but the technology's improving. He knew he would have the civil libertarians against him, as well as those who uphold the freedom to see and do what we want.'

'Once you start, where do you end?'

'My father saw that throttling all of it was a better alternative than what we have now,' Linda said.

'Have there been any threats?'

'There are always threats, but my father ignored them.'

'If he had died as a martyr, then his reforms would have been implemented.'

'As a sinner, they will not.'

'Was Helen complicit?'

'How? She was killed in the bed next to my father.'

'Helen loved James,' Violet said.

'How do you know?' Isaac said.

'I was married to James for a long time. He was infatuated with her, no doubt thought it was love. With her, it was. Whatever she may have done or been, with James, she was honest.'

***

Barry Knox knew he was implicated, if not by actual deed, then by association. He had known of the death of Ben Aberman on the night he was led away by Ugly Pete and his associates, ultimately forcing Gus, his former doorman, to become an accessory to murder. Knox knew that Gus was not a murderer, never had been. He had been guilty of unjustifiable violence, but that was how the man operated. And strip clubs needed someone strong enough to deal with a group of men out on the town, determined to get drunk, and then believing that the girls on the stage were offering more than was available.

Knox knew the police were not fools, and, if it were not for the murders, the club's activities would be investigated further. Then they would find the videos of the customers with the girls, the profits from selling them on the internet, the fact that most of the girls were selling themselves, and he was their pimp. He made a phone call to someone who understood.

'I can't protect you for much longer,' Knox said. 'If Helen hadn't been killed, no one would have ever known about Aberman, and nobody would have visited this club.'

'Why are you calling me now? That was never agreed to.'

'Am I the only one living who knows the truth?'

'You'll not speak.'

'Why?'

'You only live as long as you are of use.'

'And what use am I?'

'I may have need of you in the future.'

'That was the last time, I told you that before.'

'If I go down, you go down, and I know of your history, what you are capable of. You were put in that club to ensure the truth was never revealed. You have served your purpose well, but you are not indispensable.'

'What about Gus? He did what was expected, but he's in jail.'

'He was never important. Knox, don't call me again. If I need you, you'll be contacted.'

Knox walked around the club, surveyed his domain. He had enjoyed it once, but now he despised it, and all on account of one man. He knew his life was forfeit if he stayed, but how could he leave? Wasn't that how they operated, those who had killed Aberman and the others? Hidden behind the scenes, nameless, while others did their dirty work, suffered for them. If he went to the police with what he knew, what could they do? They could not protect him, not totally, and there were crimes he was answerable for, crimes they would not turn a blind eye to. He walked backed to his office. The club was due to open in another hour, and his new doorman did not know the ropes yet. He needed training.

***

Wendy Gladstone had not been satisfied with Ben Aberman's widow's reason for being at the house in Bray. She decided to visit her at her home in Chelsea. She found the woman in a good mood.

'I've secured the house in Bray,' Christine Aberman said.

'It's a good job his body was found,' Wendy said. She had had a restless night with arthritis and was not in the mood for polite conversation.

'This house has been good to us, but my husband, he wants the quiet life, the same as I do, and with its sale, we'll be able to retire. I may even join in some of the village activities.'

'How long have you known that your husband was dead?'

'Ever since you found his body.'

'How long have you suspected?'

'For a few years. Our marriage ended, but it wasn't acrimonious. He used to keep in touch on an occasional basis, birthday card, that sort of thing, and then nothing.'

'You didn't approach the police with your concerns?'

'What did I have? The former owner of a strip joint has disappeared. What would you have done?'

'His disappearance would have been registered as a missing person.'

'Exactly, and then, even if the police were interested, there'd be the dumb questions. Why did a strip club owner disappear? What makes you think he's dead? Was he involved in drug dealing, prostitution, illegal sex-trafficking? My husband would not appreciate questions being asked about his wife's first husband.'

'You did nothing.'

'There was nothing I could do. I still regarded Ben as a friend, but he had become an absent friend. In time, I forgot about him and moved on with my life.'

'All the time knowing there was a house in Bray for you.'

'It wasn't that important. This house is paid off, we're not short of money, and what if I had tried to declare him dead?'

'The questions you were worried about,' Wendy said.

'If he hadn't been found, we would have stayed living here. It's a bit like winning the lottery. Before you win it, you survive. Afterwards, you wonder how you managed to live before.'

'Slater, what can you tell me about him?'

'We knew him, used him to purchase the house. Apart from that, not a lot. He'd sometimes come to the house in Bray, came to one or two of the parties, enjoyed himself.'

'Did Slater take advantage of the women?'

'He did.'

'And it didn't concern you?'

'I was younger then, less critical.'

'Was Daisy one of the women?'

'She was there a few times, never Helen, if that's what you're going to ask.'

'We know that Slater was present when your husband was murdered. Did you have any suspicions the man was crooked?'

'No.'

'You're a smart woman. You're at a party with drunken men, whores. You must have formed an opinion.'

'I knew the sort of men Ben associated with. He was not a dishonest man, but he was involved in a dishonourable profession. Slater, he was involved in shady deals, I know that.'

'How?'

'Ben told me.'

'Anything more?'

'No more than that. I didn't want the details.'

Wendy could see the woman was not comfortable with discussing her past life. If she had been an innocent bystander, then why be nervous? If she was involved, then why deny it? Associating with criminals, ensuring there were women available, may not have been everyone's idea of a party in the countryside, but it wasn't necessarily illegal.

'You're holding back,' Wendy said. 'You couldn't be married to a man for so many years and not be aware of what he was up to, who he was associating with.'

'I can't say any more.'

'Can't? Are you being threatened?'

'It's hard to explain.'

'I've got all day,' Wendy said.

'Ben was associating with the wrong kind of people, I could see that. At first, the men at the parties were the same as Ben. Purely interested in having a good time, running clubs. At the last party I attended, this was three years before he disappeared, there had been an argument between Ben and another man. He had turned up at the door, and he wasn't there for a good time.'

'Who do you think it was?'

'I had no idea at the time. He was well-dressed in a suit, in his late fifties. Apart from that, there's not a lot I can tell you. The two men went into another room, Slater joined them, not that he was happy as he had been occupied in another room with one of the women. Thirty minutes later, all three men emerged, and they're cheerful.'

'Then what?'

'Slater goes back to the woman, and the mysterious man leaves.'

'What did Ben say?'

'A minor dispute, that's all.'

'But you didn't believe him.'

'That's when I knew he was in too deep. That's when I decided not to attend any more parties.'

'Did you ever meet Helen?'

'Never. I knew he was playing the field, but I never knew who, and that's the truth.'

'This man you saw with your husband and Slater, does he frighten you?'

'I remember his eyes. They were cold. He was an attractive man, not like some of the others. He was a man used to people doing what he wanted. He could have killed Ben.'

'How do we find him?'

'He's dead.'

'How do you know this?'

'I know his name.'

'What was it?'

'Gerald Adamant.'

Chapter 21

The revelation of a tie-in between Helen Langdon's former husband and a former lover came as a surprise to the team in Homicide. On the one hand, was a man known for his philanthropy, on the other, a man who had criminal connections.

The team were in Isaac's office at Challis Street. 'Is she certain?' Isaac asked Wendy.

'She didn't make the connection at the time, knowing nothing about the man, other than what she had heard about him.'

'She kept this quiet from us.'

'She was the only one who saw him at the party, except for Aberman and Slater.'

'And they're both dead. She's worried she'll be next.'

'Is there another side to Gerald Adamant we don't know?' Larry said.

'The man's always come across as clean,' Isaac said. 'Bridget, what do you have?'

'Gerald Adamant, seventy-three when he died. The family money came through significant investments in Africa. It was his grandfather who made a fortune, his father who invested it wisely, and Gerald who devoted their wealth to worthy causes.'

'Has he worked? What's his education?'

'He went to Eton, then Oxford, majoring in Economics. After university, he worked as an investment analyst at the family firm, did well according to the reports. On the death of his father, he appointed someone to run the company. He was a clever man, and there are no black marks against him. He married in his thirties, Archie and Abigail the result of that union. His wife died of cancer, he married again, a woman who's twenty years younger than him. She had a child, Howard. The marriage broke down; they divorced. Howard stayed with the father; the mother took off overseas. After some years, Gerald Adamant married Helen Langdon. The rest you know.'

'We need to know what Adamant was doing with Aberman,' Larry said.

'But how? There's no one alive to tell us now,' Wendy said.

'There are Adamant's children,' Isaac said as he picked up his phone. 'Mr Adamant, we need to talk.'

'If it's important.'

'It is.'

'We can meet at the house, two hours.'

'Your sister and brother?'

'I can't answer for them. If you want them there, you can give them a call.'

'That'll not be necessary. We want to talk to each of you individually.'

Isaac and Larry arrived at the Adamants' house earlier than the two hours. Isaac parked the car on the gravel driveway and looked around him. He and Larry walked over to the expansive lawn in front of the house; a peacock strolled by.

'The upkeep must cost plenty,' Larry said.

'There's no shortage of money. I checked out the Adamants' investment company on the internet. They posted record profits at the end of the last financial year.'

'I hope this is important,' Archie Adamant said once the three of them were seated in the library.

'It is. Mr Adamant, did your father know Ben Aberman?'

'Not to my knowledge, but I wouldn't have known all his movements or all his acquaintances.'

'You know who he is?'

'I was at Helen's trial, and Aberman's been on the television. I know he was Helen's lover before she met my father.'

'Apart from a shared history through Helen, we were unaware that the two men knew each other.'

'Did they?'

'We have a witness to them meeting the one time at Aberman's house in Bray.'

'Then I can't help you. Our father never mentioned it. Is it suspicious?'

'We're not sure. Two months after their acrimonious meeting, Aberman disappears, now known to have been murdered. And Nicholas Slater, Aberman's lawyer, who was also present at their meeting, was shot in the head as he was just about to tell us who is behind the group that took over Aberman's businesses.'

'Are you implying that my father was a criminal?'

'What do you reckon? Your father could have been involved in Aberman's death. He couldn't have been involved in Slater's.'

'Are you accusing me of Slater's murder?' Adamant said.

'We're police officers. We're putting forward scenarios, evaluating reactions, exploring the possibilities.'

'You'll get no reaction from me, other than disdain that you could consider my father was involved.'

'If your father was involved with Aberman's death, you could be involved with Slater's.'

'That's illogical and insulting.'

'Why? You've got money, a good life. Maybe it's a little boring, the same as it was for your father. He met Aberman, sensed an opportunity for adventure. He'd not be the first honest person to be seduced by the glamour of crime.'

'Are you suggesting that Helen passed herself on to our father after her lover was murdered?'

'I wasn't, but it's possible. What if Helen knew about your father? What if she saw her survival in aligning with him, playing the dutiful wife? The greatest confidence trick of all time, the charming older man, the devoted younger wife. How much did they manage to scam out of your father's rich friends?'

'You cannot continue to denigrate the memory of my father with such nonsense. He loved Helen, she loved him, and as for this criminal theory, that's all it is.'

'I hope you're right. But if it's proved right, she was more calculating than we had previously thought. If her lover is killed, and she knows she's about to die as well, she then inveigles her way into your father's affections. And when she is ready, she killed your father. Did you, Mr Adamant, love her too? Don't answer. I know what it is.'

'Everyone loved her, even Howard. That's how it was with the woman.'

'And once she's got you all where she wants you, she kills your father, calls for your sister.'

'But Helen went to prison.'

'She had weighed up the options. It was either a sentence for first-degree murder or, with mitigating circumstances, it's second-degree or manslaughter. She's prepared to do her time, but along comes James Holden. He falls for her, uses his influence, and she's out in four years.'

'What sort of woman could contemplate such a thing?'

'A woman who would have made plans. And once she was out of prison, you gave her a flat, money as well. Did she sleep with you by way of thanks?'

'No. She was too good a person for that.'

'Which means you loved her, saw yourself as not worthy. Is that why you killed her? Who was it who phoned you? Daisy? The concierge?'

'This is all wrong. I'm not guilty of what you have said. As to why our father was with Aberman and Slater, I don't know,' Archie Adamant said.

***

'It's a good theory,' Larry said as he and Isaac drove away from Adamant's house.

'Can you believe that Gerald Adamant is the Mr Big of the group that took over Aberman's business and then killed him?' Isaac said.

'It's not impossible. Could Helen maintain this hatred for so long, and then kill Adamant for no return?'

'Her parents may be able to shed some insight on the woman.'

'Then we'd better go and visit them,' Larry said.

'I'll go with Wendy. She can talk to the mother,' Isaac said.

Frank and Betty Mackay were pleased when Isaac and Wendy knocked on their door. 'We've not been far since it happened,' Frank said. 'We talk about her all the time. What she had done, where she had been. It's still hard sometimes, but we battle on.'

'A cup of tea, Mrs Mackay?' Wendy said.

'Please excuse my bad manners. I'll go and put the kettle on.'

'I'll give you a hand.'

In the kitchen of the small house, Wendy took the opportunity to speak to Helen's mother. 'Mrs Mackay, we're confused. We can't decide whether your daughter is the victim of an unforeseen chain of circumstances or whether she had been manipulating them.'

'She still died in that hotel room,' the mother replied. Wendy could see that she was still emotional.

'That doesn't make sense, I'll agree, but before that, even before she started working in the Dixey Club, what was she like?'

'She was a lovely child, always cared for us. Even then, she was the one the school friends gravitated to. I can't remember how many times she had them over here, always happy, playing the music too loud.'

It was clear to Wendy that Helen Langdon's mother wanted to remember the child, not the adult, not the victim of a murderer's bullet. 'After Helen left school, where did she go?' Wendy knew, but she wanted the woman to open up.

'University, and then to an accountant's firm in London. We thought she was going to be okay.'

'What do you mean?'

'Sometimes with Helen, we couldn't be sure what she was thinking. I'd ask, only to be told, "It's nothing, Mum, nothing to worry about".'

'But you did worry.'

'Maybe if I had seen it.'

'Seen what?'

'A coldness towards people. She would be friendly, loving with us, but she could be remote at times.'

'Intelligent?'

'Exceptional. It certainly didn't come from us. She rarely studied for an exam, just seemed to breeze through.'

'Photographic memory?'

'They said it was at the school.'

'Why did she leave the accountant's and go and work in Dixey's?'

'She never attached much importance to her looks.'

'She was beautiful,' Wendy said.

'It meant nothing to her. She knew she had this ability over people, and she knew how to manipulate them.'

'Did you have problems with young men when she was in her teens?'

'We know she was sleeping with one or two of them. I questioned her once about it. She told me not to worry as she had no intention of falling pregnant or in love.'

'What did you and your husband do?'

'Apart from worry? There wasn't a lot we could do, and she never snuck a boy into the house. In fact, we never saw her with a steady boyfriend. Occasionally she'd meet one, do what she wanted, and come home.'

'No emotions from her, no sneaking in the door?'

'With Helen, she'd come in the door, tell us what she had just done, then sit down and watch the television with us. In time, we had to accept it, and she wasn't coming to any harm. She was the ideal child, never forgot our birthdays, occasionally bought me a box of chocolates.'

'After she left home?'

'She'd come home every weekend while she was at university, never brought a friend. And then she was working, doing well. After one year or thereabouts, she was on a stage.'

'How did you find out?'

'The usual. She came home, announced she was now a dancer.'

'Did she elaborate?'

'No. We were upset, but she said not to worry.'

'Did you know Ben Aberman?'

'We never met anyone, not then. We did meet Gerald Adamant and his family.'

'Did you approve?'

'Initially, no. The man was much older than Helen, but she was happy. In time, we came to accept it.'

'Your daughter was arrested for his murder. How did you and your husband react?'

'We're shocked. Helen's never shown any violence before. We drove up to where she was being held. Helen's in a cell. She said that Gerald went crazy and she had to stop him. Outside, Gerald's children. They're upset over their father's death, over Helen being charged. They can't believe she's guilty, neither can we.'

'Mrs Mackay, would you be surprised if I told you that Helen may have killed him not in self-defence but as a premeditated attack?'

'I'll never believe that of Helen.'

In the other room, Isaac spoke with Helen's father. 'Is it possible that Helen was not the innocent she portrayed herself to be?' Isaac said.

'She never portrayed herself as innocent, just a victim of circumstance.'

'What do you mean?'

'This hold she had over people.'

'Could you see through it?'

'When she was a child, I could.'

'Dixey's?'

'I went once, tried to plead with her to come home.'

'Did you see her on the stage?'

'No, I left before then. She said she was fine, life was good.'

'Did you believe her?'

'Helen had no issues with what she was doing.'

'Do you believe she was capable of love?'

'With her parents, yes. With the men, no.'

'Gerald Adamant?'

'We hoped she was, but we could never be certain.'

'We have serious doubts about their relationship, although we believe she was in love with James Holden.'

'The proof?'

'His wife said it was love. She had seen them together in Holden's office, at the Holden house.'

'Is that why they were in that room when they were shot?'

'We believe so.'

'I read about Aberman,' Helen's father said. He had initially cheered up on talking about his daughter, but now he was sad again.

'Did you meet him?'

'I met a man when I entered the club, a big man, gruff voice.'

'That's probably Gus, the doorman and bouncer. He's charged with being an accessory to Aberman's murder.'

'Is Helen involved? She always had an unusual outlook on life, a detachment. She had no concept of what was moral and what was not. She had her set of values, and that was that.'

'Did you talk to her about it?'

'When she was younger. Not that she ever caused any trouble, and her school marks were excellent. And then, there was the university and the accountant's, and then…'

'She was in a strip club,' Isaac said.

'She threw all that she had away for nothing. Did she kill Aberman?'

'Do you believe she could?'

'Helen was capable of anything, good or bad. To her, there was no difference.'

'It must be painful for you to be so honest.'

'The truth is best served by my openness. My wife will try to cover for her, but what good will it do? If Helen is guilty, it will come out eventually.'

'Helen did not kill Ben Aberman; however, Gerald Adamant's death is suspicious.'

'Whatever the truth, we'll have to deal with it,' Frank Mackay said.

Isaac could see a devastated man who had learnt to deal with the reality of his daughter. He had seen through her, but others continued to believe in her.

Chapter 22

Isaac and Wendy arrived back at Challis Street. As they entered the building, Superintendent Seth Caddick was waiting.

'It's a good job I caught you. In my office, five minutes,' Caddick said to Isaac.

'What now?' Isaac whispered to Wendy as the man walked away.

'He was smiling, it can only be good news,' Wendy said.'

'Good for who?'

Isaac walked up the stairs to the third floor, part of his keep fit regime to avoid taking the lift as much as possible.

'You've been questioning Archie Adamant, accusing him of being involved,' Caddick said as Isaac settled himself on the hard chair opposite the man's desk.

'We're reopening the case into his father's death. I was attempting to make him open up.'

'And did he?'

'Not really. There are hidden layers to this case, and Adamant knows some of them.'

'And you feel that upsetting Adamant is one way of achieving this?'

'I do. Adamant and anyone else who is not totally open.'

'He's made a complaint.'

'It's a murder enquiry. I'm not going easy on him just because his father was murdered.'

'I'm not expecting you to.'

'Then why am I here?'

'There's an audit of Homicide.'

Isaac knew it to be the expected audit of the superintendent, not the department.

'We're ready,' Isaac said.

'Not with all these murders unsolved.'

'The investigations are proceeding satisfactorily.'

'You've solved one murder. That leaves five. What about Gerald Adamant's death? Is it murder?'

'It's a theory at this time.'

Isaac sensed a change in his superintendent, a change he did not like. The man wanted a favour; he wasn't sure if he could give it, not sure how to avoid it.

'What do you need from me to solve Holden's murder?' Caddick said.

'No more than we have at present. Why are you asking?'

'Commissioner Davies has thrown me to the wolves. An unfavourable audit of Homicide will reflect badly on me.'

'It will reflect badly on us all, but where's the problem? Our record is sound, our reporting is up to date, and we, as a team, are conscious of budgetary constraints. What do you have to worry about?'

'Goddard was a good man, knew what he was doing,' Caddick said.

'That's not what you said before.'

'I understand your animosity. I'm an ambitious man, the same as you.'

'We have little in common,' Isaac said.

'If I receive a negative mark, it will reflect on you and your department.'

'You'll make sure it does.'

'Not me, not this time. I'm offering a truce, the chance to protect each other.'

'I will do my duty as a detective chief inspector. What more can I do?'

'Davies is attempting to consolidate Homicide departments, get rid of Challis Street.'

'The man never gives up.'

'He's a survivor, so am I, so is Goddard, and so are you. Any attempt to reduce staffing levels, the number of Homicide departments, will affect you as much as me.'

'Not Davies,' Isaac said.

'I know it,' Caddick replied. 'We need each other. Goddard not coming back, so we'd better come to an arrangement. If I don't present us well enough to the auditors, it's my head and your department.'

***

Ben Aberman's former wife finally had possession of the house in Bray. Before she moved in, she had the place painted inside and out. Her husband was not so keen, as he had to commute the extra distance to London each day. 'I've longed for this day for so long,' she said as he attempted to carry her over the threshold, a mock attempt at pretending it was their first night together as man and wife.

The fact that he pulled a muscle in his lower back dampened the moment. Later that day, she walked around the garden, keeping her distance from where her dead husband had been found. 'We'll cover the area with concrete, put up a pergola,' she said.

Her husband, a calm and steadying influence, only nodded. Whatever she wanted, he knew she'd get. He had not wanted to enter the house as it reignited memories in his wife, memories she had kept repressed. He had looked upstairs and into the room where Aberman had been shot. It had been a bedroom, now it would be a study for him. A reminder that Ben Aberman was dead and he was not coming back, thankfully.

***

The reopening of the investigation into the death of Gerald Adamant had certain repercussions. The majority of those who had been close to the man and to Helen would have preferred it to be left alone. There was a cherished memory of the man, a fondness for the woman, and both were flawed. Helen's flaws were all the more apparent after her murder and more so after her past life had been exposed again. Not that it was a great secret before, as she had never attempted to conceal it totally, but now the gutter press was digging in the dirt, trying to find out the salacious, interviewing those who had known her. If they couldn't get what they wanted, they made it up.

As far as the media was concerned, Helen Langdon did not gyrate on that pole at Dixey's, she was taking the men into the back room. And as for Holden, she seduced him, dragged him into that hotel, and then a jealous ex-lover, probably a criminal, had come in and in a rage of jealousy shot Helen and Holden.

The truth, Isaac knew, was what people believed. No amount of explaining the facts at a press conference, or if he agreed to an interview, would change what people thought. James Holden, as a result, regained some respectability. Many in the community believed in what he had been trying to achieve, and some were willing to admit that he had erred, not because of his weaknesses, but because societal values and the openness of modern-day England had corrupted even him.

All that Isaac knew was that his department had reached a critical juncture in the investigation. The murders appeared to have ceased, everyone's dirty linen was out in the open.

Caddick was a nuisance, now looking to Isaac and his team to get him out of trouble, and even Isaac wasn't sure what to do. Other stations, other police officers, were concerned about the consolidation of various departments, the shutting down of some stations, even reducing police numbers out on the street. Isaac knew it was a retrograde step, and even Davies couldn't do anything about it, other than take advantage to strengthen his position, weaken others.

The first that Isaac heard by way of confirmation that Richard Goddard's star was again in the ascendancy was when Bridget came bursting into his office. 'DCS Goddard's coming back.' The second was when the man put his head around the door. 'Caddick's gone,' Goddard said. One-minute Caddick was on the phone, the next he was out of the front door.

Isaac rushed over to warmly shake Goddard's hand; the others in the office, likewise.

Goddard made an impromptu speech. 'Thanks for welcoming me back. Commissioner Davies has great faith in this department, a faith that you will show is fully justified.'

'Superintendent Caddick?' Wendy asked.

'He's been assigned a position in a regional station. He will retain the rank of superintendent.'

Inside Isaac's office with the door closed, Isaac asked his senior, 'What's the truth?'

'Davies is playing for time. If he puts me here, then he's shown that he has taken notice of the criticism levelled at Caddick. He'll take the flak for removing me and others and strengthen his position, turn it to his advantage.'

'Caddick?'

'Davies has protected him. A regional station, lower responsibilities, and not subjected to the same scrutiny as we are.'

'He left in a hurry, no coming in here to say goodbye.'

'The man was thankful to be out of here. He made no friends here.'

'We'll not miss him. We can rely on you to deal with the audit.'

'I will. However, James Holden?'

'It all points to Helen Langdon as the primary target, although there were others who bore a grudge against Holden. Since then, as you well know, there have been several other murders.'

'I've kept up to date with the case,' Goddard said.

'We believe the murderer entered the hotel with another prostitute. He drugged her – she woke up later – and then walked across the passageway, entered the room, and then shot the two of them in bed.'

'The other prostitute?'

'Gwendoline. She's still alive, although her previous flatmate, Daisy, is not.'

'And Adamant?'

'In light of what's happened, what we've found out, his death is suspicious,' Isaac said. 'And Slater's and his receptionist's deaths, they could be related to Aberman.'

'Wherever Helen Langdon moved, death seemed to follow,' Goddard said.

'They're all interconnected, and just focussing on who shot the first victim is going nowhere. The man with Gwendoline is not easy to trace.'

'Any clues?'

'Nothing significant from the prostitute. The normal – average height, average weight, hat pulled forward.'

'Did anyone else see him?'

'The concierge at the hotel, but he wasn't looking either. He keeps his eyes down, takes the money off the woman and hands her the key. He had a good little number there, but he couldn't stop peeping into the rooms.'

'No more from him?'

'Nothing.'

'If Gwendoline remembered anything, she'd probably be dead now.'

'It's her only protection. The man killed two people in cold blood, and then another prostitute later; a third wouldn't concern him.'

'If he were paid for two, he'd not kill any more unless he was compromised,' Goddard said.

***

Wendy dropped in on Mrs Hawthorne, Aberman's next-door neighbour. It had become a weekly routine, and the woman always seemed to remember something on each occasion. She found her not to be her usual cheerful self.

'What's the problem?' Wendy asked as she sat down in the front room.

'It's her next door. She reckons I'm nosey, always looking over the fence. She used to be friendly in the past, but now, it's as if she's hiding something.'

Wendy thought the woman's observations were nothing more than feeling unneeded. In all the years since Aberman had disappeared, she had kept watch on his house, but now, her looking over the fence from behind a drawn curtain in an upstairs window was not wanted. Wendy left the house and walked next door.

At the front door was Ben Aberman's ex-wife. 'She's been accusing us in the neighbourhood of killing Ben,' she said. Wendy could see that the woman was agitated.

'Is that it?'

'Not totally. My husband, he's not so keen on the place. I thought it would be relaxing here, but he wants to go back to London.'

'And you?'

'I'm staying. Mrs Hawthorne, if she continues, will have a writ against her for slander. There are a few others around here who'll back me up.'

'You know some of the locals?'

'One or two. I lived here for a while, and they didn't like it when I left, and then Ben was flaunting the debauchery.'

'Debauchery?'

'You know what I'm referring to, the same as the nosey old woman next door does. This place was depraved, women everywhere, and not too fussy who was watching.'

'Ben?'

'I was told he behaved himself, not sure if that's true.'

'Who told you?'

'Some of those who attended.'

'Important people?'

'I never pried into who they were.'

'We were told Ben paid for everything.'

'He did.'

'But how? He couldn't have afforded the parties that often.'

'Every other week, regular as clockwork. Arrive at the house eight at night on Saturday, leave midday on Sunday.'

'But you attended the parties.'

'The earlier ones, but they were tame by comparison. It was only after we separated that they changed, Ben changed.'

'The people who attended?'

'I've told you all this before. Slater was there, so were some of the girls from the club. Not the one that was killed with James Holden. I told you I saw Gerald Adamant at the house once, angry as well, but that was a long time ago. Apart from that, no one I knew.'

'Your husband?'

'We met some time after. He never met Ben.'

Wendy wasn't sure where the conversation was heading. She'd been invited in, and she approved of the work that had been done in the house. It was freshly painted, and there was a pleasant feel to the house. It was hard to envisage it as a den of iniquity, but that was what it had been once.

'What about where they buried Ben?'

'We're putting a concrete slab over it.'

'No issues moving into the house, considering?'

'I'm not squeamish. My husband is.'

'I feel that you know more than you ever tell us,' Wendy said. 'You knew the people who came to the parties while you were here. Who were they?'

'Slater, my husband. The others I never knew. Barry Knox, he used to come here.'

'Gus, the doorman at Dixey's?'

'He was here, but I can't remember him taking an active part unless getting drunk qualifies.'

'Any dubious characters?'

'None that I remember.'

Wendy knew the woman was lying. She had played the game strategically. She was isolated from the parties, from the deaths, and now she was back at the house in Bray. Wendy was not sure of her innocence. She had divorced Ben Aberman several years before his death, and her life since then had been one of normality. With no more to be achieved, the police sergeant left the house and headed back to Challis Street and the police station.

Chapter 23

Barry Knox looked at the monitor in his office. He could see the club was filling up, and his decision to bring in fresh women was working. His new doorman, a tough, tattooed individual by the name of Doug, was not as good as Gus. He'd upset the women backstage on a couple of occasions by walking in and staring while they were preparing to go up on stage.

Knox had had to explain to Doug, a former bouncer at an illegal gambling club, that the women didn't mind being gawped at up on stage where they were being paid. However, backstage they hung on to their modesty for as long as they could. Knox did not elaborate that they found Doug repulsive. Gus, not the most attractive of men, had always been pleasant to the women, opening the door for them, helping them to carry their bags into the club. Doug was not.

The bed in the rear room was unused, the occasional favour from one of the women to Knox missing. A better class of women, a better return on the investment, but no more late-night romance.

Knox was pleased with the way the business was going; he was not pleased with the man sitting opposite.

'He said he knew you,' Doug said as he let the man into the office.

'Did you check him out?'

'He showed his ID.'

After Doug had left, Knox turned to Isaac. 'Are you here to ask questions? I've told you all I know.'

'Not all.'

'What do you mean?'

'Ben Aberman's ex-wife. What can you tell me about her?'

'She never came in here, and besides, when I took over, Aberman was with Helen.'

'You used to go to the parties out at Aberman's house before you took over here.'

'Sometimes. I was running another club. He invited me as a courtesy. I'd return the favour.'

'Did you have parties?'

'Not me. I didn't have that sort of money, but we swapped girls at the clubs. If one of them was off ill or absent or overdosed, we'd send one of ours over.'

'The parties at Aberman's house when his wife was there, what were they like?'

'The later parties were better.'

'Regardless, what were they like?'

'Plenty of alcohol, plenty of women.'

'Did his wife take part?'

'Not that I saw. Mind you, I was always busy.'

Yet again, Isaac realised that the ex-Mrs Aberman was somehow involved. She had always given the impression of non-involvement in her husband's business affairs, yet she attended the parties, even turned a blind eye to the shenanigans.

'Aberman used to throw a lot of money around. These parties couldn't have been cheap.'

'That was Aberman. He always liked to put on a show. I never understood how he did it, but I was glad of the invite.'

'You went to every one?'

'Not all of them. We weren't that friendly, it was just business.'

'Gerald Adamant, what can you tell me about him?'

'Not much, apart from him marrying Helen. After she left here, nobody heard from her for a few months, and then, all of a sudden, she's being squired around the town on Adamant's arm. The first time Daisy saw her picture in a newspaper, she was in here showing me.'

'Daisy, was she surprised?'

'Daisy and Helen, they'd been sort of friends in the club, although, with Helen, you never knew if she was a friend or whether it was something else.'

'What do you mean?'

'I'm not sure how to explain it. She came to the club, got up on the stage, and she was a great performer. She knew how to excite the men, and then she'd finish for the night, get dressed in regular clothes and walk out of the door.'

'What else?'

'Before she moved in with Aberman on a semi-permanent basis, no one knew where she went after she left the club.'

'You know a lot about this woman,' Isaac said.

'Not me, but there she is with Adamant, and then she marries the man. There was plenty of gossip about her. Most of the girls here on that pole, they're looking for the knight in shining armour, ready to take them away from all this and into a life of luxury, the loving husband, the house in the country. Normal childhood dreams, but with them, they carried on into adulthood. It's the life they lead, I suppose.'

'Do you want out?'

'A regular job, plenty of money? Of course I do. What do you think I'm doing here, living on the edge, wondering when the next gangster is coming to knock on the door, to tell me my number's up?'

'Is that likely?'

'Who knows. We're strictly legal here, but our protection comes at a cost.'

'Who owns this club? It's never been explained.'

'As I've told you before, a consortium of businessmen.'

'But you must have met them?'

'Not me. I've met the man who put me in this job, but apart from that, I haven't, and that's the truth.'

'I'm interested in Gerald Adamant. How did he come to know Helen?'

'I'm not sure. Some of the women said he used to come into the club.'

'Gus?'

'He said he did, but I wouldn't place too much credence on him.'

174

'Why?'

'Gus only sees the people of a night time when it's dark.'

'I need to meet this consortium,' Isaac said.

'They'll not talk to you, even if you can find them.'

'Why?'

'They're secretive.'

'Why are they secretive? You're legal.'

'Social stigma. Businessmen are after a good return on their money, and these clubs can be money in the bank, only it doesn't look good on their financial returns. It won't help their reputations, their being involved in strip clubs, prostitution, drug dealing.'

'You said there was no prostitution or drugs here.'

'There isn't, but people always associate these places with crime and sin.'

'How do you see it?'

'A night out with the boys, a chance to get drunk, to have a laugh and a look at the women. We're entertainment for the grown-ups.'

***

Back at Challis Street Police Station, Isaac called the team into his office. Chief Superintendent Goddard came as well, although he did not stay long. He gave the obligatory words of encouragement and left hurriedly, another meeting, another chance to press the flesh.

'Wendy, anything more?' Isaac said. He was sitting upright, his arms resting on his desk.

'I'm not sure I understand Ben Aberman's widow. Before, at her house in Chelsea, she was pleasant. Now, out at Bray, there's a hardness in her. She's fallen out with the next-door neighbour, accused her of prying.'

'Was she?'

'Probably.'

'You think the ex-Mrs Aberman is hiding something.'

'Yes, I do.'

'Bridget, what do we have on her?'

'Christine Aberman, married to Ben for fifteen years, no children. Originally trained as a nurse, although she's not worked for the last twenty years. She's from London, the same area as Aberman. She divorced Aberman, moved in with William Ecclestone, a bank manager, although she still uses Aberman as her surname. The house in Chelsea is beyond a bank manager's salary.'

'It was part of the divorce settlement, according to her,' Wendy said.

'It was. I have a copy of it, as well as the division of the assets,' Bridget said. 'There was no money owing on the house.'

'Could he have made this amount of money with Dixey's and two other clubs?' Larry said.

'His tax returns indicate he could not, although I assume there's a lot of black money.'

'Would he be subject to a tax audit?' Wendy said.

'Unlikely,' Isaac said. 'He'd use smart accountants to head them off, and his records would be meticulous.'

'They are,' Bridget said.

'And the house in Bray?'

'Yet again, paid off.'

'It's still suspicious,' Isaac said.

'He may have inherited money.'

'Would Aberman's ex-wife know?'

'Maybe. We could ask her.'

'Wendy, set it up. I'll go with you,' Isaac said. 'Before we wrap up, what about the consortium that took over Aberman's assets?'

'I can't make the connection to anyone. Slater was their mouthpiece.'

'He's dead, but the clubs are still running. Who are they reporting to?'

'Barry Knox would know,' Larry said.

'It's possible, but he's not talking, or he's scared.'

Chapter 24

Christine Aberman did not appreciate the visit by Isaac and his sergeant so soon after the previous visit. She was in the garden. As Wendy walked out to meet her, she glanced around at the house next door. She was sure the curtains had moved in the window that Mrs Hawthorne used for spying.

'You've ended up a very wealthy woman. Why have you kept both houses?' Wendy said.

'Good fortune, I suppose,' the woman said as she got up from her sitting position on the ground.

'It's more than that. The men who took your husband's clubs would not have hesitated to take this house. We've always assumed it was because Helen Langdon had some relationship with them, but it could be you.'

'I resent your aspersions. I was a loyal wife to Ben, even when he bought the first club. I didn't approve back then, I don't approve now. If this house and the one in Chelsea are the results of those places, then some good has come of them, but that's all.'

'Was Gerald Adamant at the parties more than the one time?'

'I told you I saw him here the one time.'

'Soon the pieces will fall into place. If we find out you're lying, it will reflect badly on you. I suggest you tell us what you know before it is too late.'

'Okay, Adamant sometimes came to the parties. I never saw him with any of the women.'

'But Adamant is known as a philanthropist,' Wendy said.

'He wasn't back then. Maybe he distanced himself afterwards, but he was up to no good when I met him.'

'Tell us about him.'

'He was a charming man, very polite. He'd come to the parties, not every time, and he and Ben would sit down and talk. Back then, they were friends, or they appeared to be.'

'What do you mean?'

'Adamant had my husband killed.'

'Are you certain?'

'It's the only explanation. I knew Ben had taken up with Helen and he was even considering marrying her.'

'How do you know this?'

'We were divorced, but we kept in contact. He phoned to tell me about Helen, told me she was a good woman.'

'Did he tell you about her working in the club?'

'He tried to explain that she was a free spirit.'

'Did you believe him?'

'I believed it was what he thought, but he was naïve. If she was wrapping herself around a pole with no clothes on, she was more than a free spirit.'

'What did you think she was?'

'I didn't think anything. Ben was keen on her, and there's no way I was going to dissuade him. Anyway, three weeks later, he's dead.'

'Do you believe that Gerald Adamant was involved with the group that took over Ben's clubs?'

'He was the group.'

'This house?'

'Slater phoned me, asked if I'd accept the house for not asking too many questions.'

'And you agreed?'

'Yes. I had committed no crime.'

'Did you believe Ben to be dead?'

'I was told he had gone overseas, and that he'd be back one day, but I didn't believe it. I didn't know he was buried in this garden.'

'Why didn't you move in?'

'That was the deal. Helen would look after the place for Aberman, maintain the pretence that he was coming back. If I had moved into the house, it would have been suspicious, and one thing Adamant did not want was anything obvious.'

'The philanthropy of the man?'

'Gerald Adamant used his charitable causes as the perfect cover. The man enjoyed living on the edge, being smarter than the next man. And then Helen kills him, claims it's self-defence, even got Adamant's children to act as character witnesses.'

'Who's running Adamant's criminal enterprises now?'

'Why are you asking me? Talk to Barry Knox, he'll know.'

***

The revelations of Christine Aberman had cleared the way forward for Homicide.

'Bridget, what do we have on Adamant's children that we didn't know before?' Isaac asked.

'Archie, the eldest. He's forty-three. Then there's Abigail, forty-one, and Howard, the younger son, the child of Gerald's second wife, he's twenty-nine.'

'Discount Howard,' Isaac said.

'Any reason?' Larry said.

'Too young.'

'But he's smart. The man can achieve plenty with a computer.'

'Okay. Leave him in for now. Let's focus on Archie.'

'Archie, short for Archibald, is a lawyer, practises in Paddington. He takes care of the family's business interests.'

'Any evidence that Archie could have taken over his father's criminal interests?'

'Is Christine Aberman's testimony enough to convince us that Gerald Adamant was behind the takeover of Aberman's clubs?' Larry said.

'It's the missing link that ties Aberman and Adamant, and Helen to Adamant. Helen knew that Adamant ordered Aberman's death. She knows where he is and she lays in a plan to snare the man.'

'But why wait so long before killing him?'

'Helen's smart. She knows that if she had killed him before they were married, then it's murder. If she married him, then killed him on their wedding night, then it's the same. But she waits, redeems herself in society.'

'It worked,' Wendy said.

'A remarkable woman,' Isaac said.

'Do you think so?' Bridget said.

'To achieve what she did, even if it was murder. She kept focussed all those years, never once letting her guard drop, and then she killed the man who had killed Aberman.'

'Do you think she loved him?' Wendy said.

'We'll never know.'

'We need to prove that Gerald Adamant was responsible for Aberman's death,' Isaac said. 'Larry, we'll go and visit his daughter. She may be the easiest to deal with.'

***

Abigail Adamant, a woman who did little other than spend the family money on frivolities, had not been easy to find. In the end, Bridget found her through accessing her Facebook account; she was at a restaurant in Chelsea.

'Miss Adamant, the death of your father's widow,' Isaac said once he and Larry had separated the woman from her friends.

'Call me Abigail,' she said. She was fashionably dressed, and also slightly drunk after lunch with her friends. One or two of them had looked over at the tall, dark and handsome detective chief inspector when Isaac and Larry had entered the restaurant. Isaac had seen the sniggering, the comments passed between the women. He had felt embarrassed. He was on duty and anxious to conclude the current investigations.

'Abigail, was your father involved in crime?'

'Are you accusing him?'

Isaac realised his questioning was probably too direct for a woman unsteady on her feet. He ordered her a black coffee. He needed her sober.

'We've received information that your father was involved in the takeover of Ben Aberman's clubs.'

'Ben Aberman?'

'Are you saying you've not heard of the man?'

'I read the news. His body was found in the back garden of his house.'

'He was the former lover of your father's widow. You must have known this.'

'Not from Helen.'

'We have to consider the possibility that Helen, a woman that no one seems to know fully, had married your father as a means of getting close enough to kill him.'

'By why marry him? Why pretend to love him and to take an interest in his causes?'

'Because if she managed to convince you and your brothers that she loved your father, you would all support her assertion that it was self-defence.'

'But it's absurd. No one could keep up that pretence for so long.'

'She could. She had stripped in a club, yet came away unscathed, she had married your father, and then she fell in love with James Holden.'

'Love?'

'His widow believes she had fallen in love with her husband.'

'Could it have been a pretence with James Holden?'

'Did you know the man?'

'He and my father were friends.'

'If we prove that your father was involved in crime, what would you think of your father?'

'Nothing would change. He did a lot of good with his causes.'

'So did James Holden, and he was killed. There's something else.'

'What is it?'

'We believe your father gave the order for Ben Aberman to be killed,' Isaac said.

'What right do you have to besmirch my father's good name by such accusations?'

'Ben Aberman and your father met on several occasions. Your father was far from the saint you would portray him as.'

'I've not said he was a saint.'

'Did you know Nicholas Slater?'

'Yes, I met him once or twice. Father introduced me to him.'

'He was an acquaintance of Ben Aberman, even went to his parties.'

'My father went to one or two, I know that.'

'Did you know what sort of parties they were?'

'I never asked my father, but I can imagine. Alcohol and a good time.'

'And women supplied by Aberman,' Isaac said.

'Good for my father, if that was the case,' Abigail said.

Larry observed Isaac going easy on the woman. 'Abigail, if what we have been told is correct, it would destroy your father's reputation,' he said.

'It wouldn't concern me. I'm not filled with the need to help others. I'm a selfish person. My father helped a lot of people. My brother is trying to do the same, but he'll not succeed as well as our father.'

'Why?'

'Our father had genuine compassion. He was charismatic, people instinctively liked him. You've met my brother. He can be blunt with people, and he doesn't have the same level of commitment. My brother and I, we're the generation that loses the money.'

'Howard, your younger brother?'

'He was never spoilt by the wealth.'

Isaac could tell that Abigail Adamant was incapable of any great passion. She did not concern herself with right and wrong, only with what gave her pleasure, and whereas she had shown compassion for Helen, she was not interested in whether her father had died as a result of murder or of a woman defending herself. Isaac had to admit that he did not like her very much.

Chapter 25

Two things happened the day following Isaac and Larry's conversation with Abigail Adamant. The first was Richard Goddard coming into Isaac's office to tell him that the audit into the department had been cancelled: it was not unexpected.

'The man beat them again,' Goddard said. 'Even the head of Counter Terrorism Command is back in his old job.'

'It's an admission from Davies that he was wrong.'

'That's not how Davies operates. He'll take the criticism, turn it into an advantage. The commissioner is a man who listens to the rank and file, a man who believes in an open-door policy to his office. The next time you meet him, he'll be friendly, singing your praises.'

'And I'm meant to show him the necessary respect?' Isaac said.

'You'll show him due deference as befits his rank.'

'The plan to remove him has been shelved?'

'It's always there, but he'll stay, at least until his contract is up. I have to give the man his due, he knows how to play the game.'

'The damage he's caused to the Met,' Isaac said.

'It's minor. We're still here, so are the majority of the competent and dedicated.'

The second thing that happened was when Abigail Adamant went home and questioned her brother, Archie.

'I was told our father was involved in Ben Aberman's murder,' Abigail said. She was sitting in the living room of the Adamant house. To one side of her was Howard, his feet hanging over the arm of the sofa. Archie sat square on, his tie loosened, his top shirt button undone.

'So what?' was Howard's reply.

'Did you know about this? Abigail said to Archie.

'Aberman was being difficult. Someone had to deal with him,' Archie replied. He resented being questioned by his sister.

'Are you condoning murder?'

'It's unproven, and since when did you care about our father as long as you had sufficient money to squander?'

'If our father killed Ben Aberman, could Helen have murdered our father?'

Howard turned around from where he had been feigning disinterest and placed his feet on the ground. 'We've been through this before. We supported Helen. If we let the police suspect we have doubts, they'll believe what Abigail has just said about our father.'

'They believe it already,' Abigail said. 'Archie, what is the truth?'

'Our father may have had another side to him. There are some discrepancies in his finances, large sums of money going in, going out.'

'Did Helen know this?'

'I don't know.'

'Did you know about our father when he was alive?' Howard asked.

'Not totally. I knew about the parties at Aberman's house. But that was a long time ago.'

'How?'

'He wanted to talk one day. He admired people such as Aberman, not concerned about their reputations, what people thought of them.'

'Was our father a crook?'

'He was a businessman who lent money.'

'High risk, high interest?'

'To people such as Ben Aberman. Our father enjoyed the subterfuge.'

'You've not answered the question,' Abigail said. 'Did our father kill Ben Aberman?'

'Not personally, but it's possible,' Archie said.

'And since then, Helen's killing of our father?'

'I still believe Helen's account of what happened,' Archie said.

'Archie, did you kill Helen?'

'I've not been responsible for any murders.'

Howard Adamant looked over at his stepbrother. He wasn't sure what to believe. Abigail sat down resignedly and looked into space. Her only concern, the impact the truth would have on her lifestyle.

***

Ten o'clock in the morning, and in Homicide the team were focussing on their individual activities. Bridget was dealing with the administration, Wendy and Larry were working on their weekly reports. Isaac was in his office checking his emails.

None of them expected Gwendoline, Daisy's former flatmate, to walk in the door. Wendy saw her first and went over. 'I had to come,' the prostitute said.

'Take a seat and take your time,' Wendy said. 'That's a nasty cut you've got there.'

'It was him,' the woman said. Wendy could see that she had slept rough the night before. Her clothes were in disarray, her hair was tangled, and the handbag she carried was open.

'Him?'

'The man who drugged me when the two were killed in the hotel.'

'What happened?'

'I'm looking at him. There's something familiar, but I can't make out what it is. I've got my money, he's had what he wanted, and I'm ready to go. He's holding my arm. I finally remember who he is. I'm frightened, trying to get free, but he's hanging on. I grabbed a knife from my bag and stabbed him.'

'When was this?'

'Last night. I've been keeping out of sight until now.'

'The cut on your arm?'

'He lashed out at me as I ran out of the room. I caught my arm on something sharp.'

Bridget came in and administered first aid. Wendy gave Gwendoline a hot drink and attempted to calm her.

'Where is he now?'

'I've no idea, and I'm scared to go home. I phoned my flatmate not to go there either, but I doubt if she listened to me.'

'Would he have your address?'

'Some of the contents of my handbag fell out. I can't find some of my cards, one of them has an address on it.'

'The address?'

'15 Brixham Street, Shepherd's Bush, Flat 5,' Gwendoline said.

Wendy made a phone call. 'There's a police car on the way to check it out. You should have come in here earlier.'

'I was frightened. He's killed two people, three if I include Daisy. He could have killed me.'

'Did he take you to that room to kill you?'

'I don't think he recognised me. Before I had red hair, now it's blonde. He wanted me for sex, that's all.'

'Describe the man?'

'I told you before, I don't look. I only do it for the drugs.'

'What do you remember?'

'He smelt nice.'

'Perfume?'

'Aftershave. He was dressed smartly.'

'A suit?'

'Yes, although I don't remember a tie.'

'Anything else?'

'The man, nothing. Maybe you think I'm lying, but I'm not. I never remember them after they've left.'

'You'd recognise the smell again?'

'I think so.'

'Very well. Let's get you cleaned up and fed. After that, we can go and see if we can find what the aftershave was.'

Isaac and Larry, realising that Wendy would be the best person to talk to Gwendoline, left her alone. After the woman had eaten breakfast at a café across the road, she and Wendy walked back to the police station. 'I wanted to join the police when I was younger,' the woman said.

'What happened?'

'Drugs. I tried them once, and I was hooked. There's nothing that can be done.'

'With treatment, it may be possible.'

'That's the problem. They give you the methadone, the counselling needed. After that, it's up to the individual to deal with the problem, but the craving, it never goes away.' Wendy, even though she had been nearly two years without a cigarette, still savoured the smell on the street. Wendy knew that heroin was different, and it had destroyed Gwendoline, a woman in her mid-thirties.

Wendy received a phone call. 'Are you certain?' she said.

She then called in Isaac and Larry. 'Gwendoline's flatmate, she's dead,' Wendy said. Gwendoline sat quietly sobbing.

'Wendy, look after Gwendoline,' Isaac said. 'I'll go with Larry to the address.'

'We need to identify the aftershave the man was wearing,' Wendy said.

'Forensics can probably do that if the smell is at the flat,' Larry said.

'Maybe, but it'll help Gwendoline if she's occupied. The man's experienced at killing. He'll not make mistakes with the flatmate. He didn't expect to meet Gwendoline again. He wasn't prepared.'

'She wasn't a bad flatmate, not as bad as Daisy,' Gwendoline said sadly. 'I must be jinxed. Share a flat with me, end up dead.'

***

Neither Isaac nor Larry were impressed with what constituted a flat for two heroin-addicted prostitutes. It was on the second floor of an old council block. The general area was not good either. In the flat, an old kitchen – two of the cupboard doors hanging off their hinges, a cooker that looked as though it had not been used for some time, a refrigerator which hummed loudly. In one corner of the main living area, an old television was switched to one of the shopping channels.

'Where's the body?' Gordon Windsor, the CSE, said as he entered with his team.

'In the other room. We've not been in there yet.'

'And you won't be until you kit up. I don't want you making a mess of the place, destroying the evidence.'

'We know the rules,' Larry said.

Inside the bedroom, a woman was sprawled across the bed. 'She's been shot,' Windsor said.

'We believe it's the same person who killed Helen Langdon and James Holden.'

'If that's the case, there'll not be much evidence.'

'The man's rattled. He hadn't expected to be recognised by the prostitute he'd drugged before.'

Isaac looked around the room: no fairy lights, no massage oil, no sign that the woman brought men back to the flat. On a bedside table stood a photo of a family. Isaac assumed it was of the woman's family in a happier time. A picture of the dead woman and two others, one of them Gwendoline, was taped to the wall.

'Not much to see here,' Windsor said.

'Any observations?'

'She's been shot at close range. There's a sign of a struggle, not much damage to the place. The bullet is probably a 9 mm.'

'The same gun that killed Langdon and Holden?'

'That's up to Forensics, not me.'

On the way out, Isaac and Larry looked into Gwendoline's room. It was the same as the other woman's, devoid of anything other than a bed, a few personal items, a few photos. Isaac picked up some clothes and toiletries, at Wendy's request. Gwendoline was at the police station, and she would not be coming back to the flat. It was a murder scene, and it now represented the best chance to find out the identity of the murderer.

Outside on the street, the usual gathering of onlookers. One of the women standing in the crowd, in her forties, overweight, blotched face, came over. 'I saw him,' she said.

Isaac pulled her to one side. 'What can you tell us?'

'I was waiting at my door for a friend,' she said. Isaac knew she was another prostitute and she had been waiting for a client.

'Your name?'

'Professional or my correct name?'

'Both.' The onlookers, sensing additional gossip, attempted to follow. A uniformed constable kept them behind the temporary barrier.

'Delilah, a hint of forbidden delights,' the woman said. It was clear she had retained a sense of humour.

'Your real name?'

'Mary Alton.'

'Miss Alton, what can you tell us.'

'Call me Delilah. Why don't you treat me to a cup of tea and something to eat? Then we can talk.'

Isaac and Larry hoped it wasn't a con job to get them to buy her a meal.

Inside the restaurant, not far from the murder scene, the three of them sat. A disinterested waiter took the order. Isaac thought the place looked unhygienic. Larry and the woman ordered fish and chips. Isaac settled for coffee only.

'Is she dead?' Delilah said.

'She's been shot.'

'I can't say I knew her. I'd occasionally hear her and her friend coming home, but apart from that, we didn't talk much. I went into their flat once to borrow something or other, I can't remember what.'

Alcohol, Isaac thought but did not comment.

'Gwendoline was okay, the other one could be snooty.'

'Snooty?'

'She thought she was better than us. Supposedly she had grown up in a posh house somewhere. She spoke well, I'll grant her that.'

'You saw the man who shot her,' Larry said.

'I'm waiting for a friend.'

'Client or friend?' Isaac said.

'One and the same. If they've got the money, they're my friend. I've got my door open, just slightly, enough to see who's coming up the stairs. My flat is near theirs. I can see it's not him, so I close my door.'

'Did he see you?'

'No. He would have killed me if I had, wouldn't he?'

'It seems probable.'

'I heard him knock on the door opposite and Annie opening it. That was the name I knew her by, probably not her real name, but most of us, we don't want to remember where we came from.'

'What happened then?' Larry said.

'Annie, she opens the door, and the man enters.'

'You're watching?'

'Not then, but I can hear well enough. The man's looking for Gwendoline, but she's not there. I can tell he's angry and Annie's not saying much.'

'Suspicious?'

'Where I live? The building is full of people like me, like him. If someone's screwing or arguing, I just turn up the music in my flat.'

'Tell us about the man?'

'He's average, nothing special, although he wore a distinctive aftershave.'

'You could smell it?'

'My friend arrived after a few minutes. He thought I'd just had another man in my flat.'

'Did it worry him?'

'He doesn't like it. He's a regular, you see. Sometimes they get jealous, but that's his problem.'

'Did you see the face of the man who entered Annie's flat?'

'Not really. He had on a heavy coat, the collar turned up. He was wearing a hat.'

'It's the same man,' Isaac said to Larry.

'Delilah, you've had a narrow escape,' Larry said.

Chapter 26

Wendy took Gwendoline shopping to try to identify the aftershave the man had been wearing. At the first shop they visited, no success. At the second, the same result. At the third, the smell of the aftershave was unmistakable. Wendy purchased a bottle and then returned to the station, but not before the two women had stopped at a restaurant.

'Not point in skimping on the budget. You're a witness. It's important we look after you,' Wendy said.

'You've been very generous,' Gwendoline said.

Wendy felt sad for the woman, a woman like so many others, just surviving day to day.

Back at the office, Isaac handed Gwendoline a small case with some of her belongings from her flat.

'When can I get the rest?' she asked.

'Wendy will organise it for you. Maybe tomorrow. Do you have somewhere to stay?'

'I've a friend, she'll look after me for a few days.'

'I'll take her there,' Wendy said.

'When you get back, we need to discuss what we have,' Isaac said.

'It's a bit obvious, wearing aftershave,' Larry said.

'The man wasn't expecting to meet Gwendoline. He's flustered, realising his cover's been broken. Whoever he is, he must be one of the men we've been interviewing. Anyone that comes to mind?'

'Archie Adamant, he's a smart dresser, his brother's not.'

'John Holden, when he was alive, may have qualified, but he's dead and buried.'

'I had him down as the possible murderer, but if Gwendoline's correct, it can't be him.'

Wendy returned to the office twenty minutes after dropping off Gwendoline. 'It's a better place than Daisy's was,' she said.

'Housekeeping is not Gwendoline's strong point. The flat she shared with the last murder victim was a mess, even worse than my place,' Isaac said.

'I suppose you don't have stray men over at your place,' Wendy said.

'No strays of any kind.'

'Coming back to the point,' Larry said, 'the only men we've met who are still free are Barry Knox, although I can't remember him smelling of anything, Christine Aberman's current husband, and the two Adamant men. It still doesn't explain who shot Slater and his receptionist, and ruined my best suit.'

'It's been dry cleaned, returned to you,' Isaac said.

'I know, but it's not the same. The blood of two dead people has been on it.'

'You're becoming squeamish.'

'Maybe, but we were there when they were shot. If we'd been in the line of fire, it would have been us that day.'

'Now's not the time to indulge in retrospection. We've got a man out there that we need to find, and fast. Discount Howard Adamant for now, and besides, he's a young man about town, he'll have no trouble finding female companionship.'

'No need of Gwendoline,' Wendy said.

'Focus on the more likely candidates.'

'I've always found Mrs Aberman's second husband to be a little strange.'

'Is it possible?' Isaac said.

'Everyone seems to tie into everyone else. Aberman and Adamant were interconnected. Maybe her second husband is as well.'

'What about Slater?'

'What about him?'

'It was a difficult shot. Could there be more than one murderer?'

'We've got Ugly Pete and Gus for Aberman's death. Nobody for Slater's but neither Ugly Pete nor Gus has any history with guns,' Larry said.

'We've always said the murders of Helen Langdon and James Holden were professional. What do we have on Archie Adamant? Any history of military training, any experience with weapons?' Isaac said.

The team dispersed. Isaac and Larry left to go and visit Archie Adamant, Wendy to check on Gwendoline, to see if she remembered anything more.

Adamant was not pleased to see the two police officers. He was in his office at the house. He was a sombre man, devoid of any humour. His stepbrother took life as it came, made plenty of money and enjoyed himself. Archie looked as if enjoyment was alien to him.

'Is this important?' Archie said. He was sitting down, aiming to look relaxed, not achieving it.

Isaac sniffed the air – nothing. He liked to splash on aftershave, especially if he had a date, but it had been a few weeks since his last one. The woman had seemed pleasant, but on the night of the date she found out that he appreciated a good steak and a glass of wine, whereas she was vegetarian and drank a glass of water. The evening had ended badly, although she had phoned up afterwards to apologise, agreeing that maybe she had been a little sensitive. Isaac knew there would not be a next time.

'Mr Adamant, are you in the habit of visiting prostitutes?' Isaac said.

'How dare you come in here and accuse me of such a thing.'

'We'll need to conduct a search of your house. A warrant is being prepared.'

Larry sat quietly and watched his DCI bait the man. A search warrant for the man's house was not in preparation, and even if it were, it would be up to Homicide to show just reason for it to be issued.

'Yesterday a man paid for the services of a prostitute. That man was also with her in the room opposite to Helen Langdon and James Holden when they were murdered. You, Mr Adamant, fit the description of that man. How are you with weapons? Have you had any training? Will we find any firearms at your house?'

'I'm proficient with firearms. However, I've not visited Gwendoline or whatever her name is.'

'You're not married,' Larry said.

'What's that got to do with it?' Adamant took stock of what he was saying. He did not want the police searching his house with a warrant, concerned that a closer inspection into his business dealings would be detrimental. 'Okay, bring a team to the house. Check what you want and do it now.'

Larry did not need to call for a team. He was more than capable of conducting a detailed search. He checked the bathrooms of the house, the bedrooms, even Howard's. After thirty minutes he returned. 'All clear,' he said.

Isaac was in the other room talking to Howard, Archie's younger brother. 'I'll let Archie know,' Howard said.

Larry noticed that Howard had smartened himself up and he had shaved. 'I've an appointment with a bank,' Howard said. 'I've already told DCI Cook. I've been offered a contract to write an anti-hacking program for them.'

'Your expertise?'

'If you can hack as well as I can, you can also put in place the safeguards. It's big money for me. I may even move out of here, buy my own place.'

'This house is magnificent,' Isaac said.

'It's time to go. Archie can be a pain in the rear end, and Abigail, she turns her nose up when I bring a woman back with me.'

'She seems broadminded.'

'She is, but she disapproves that it's always a different one.'

'What's the problem with Archie?' Isaac asked.

'He had a touch of the prostate, can't get it up.'

'Incapable of maintaining an erection?'

'That's why he's grumpy. The man's in his forties, at his peak, and he's finished. All he's got is his work and a miserable attitude. Me, I'm at my best. Plenty of money, plenty of women.'

Isaac and Larry knew that if Archie could not consummate a sexual relationship, then he was not guilty of murdering Helen Langdon and James Holden. Gwendoline had made it clear that the man she had been with had had sexual intercourse with her.

***

Barry Knox sat in the office at Dixey's. It was two in the afternoon, and the place was quiet, apart from a cleaner out the front sweeping the floor and another polishing the pole in the centre of the stage. Behind the bar, the barman checked everything was ready, placing last-minute orders to the alcohol supplier. Around the back, in the dressing room, none of the women was present; most wouldn't be in the club until after seven in the evening.

Isaac and Larry walked through the club. The new doorman did not need to check their identification; he knew them on sight. They knew him, as well, having already checked him out back at the police station. Doug Maybury had served two years for the violent beating of a man, and for extortion.

'Not again,' Knox said when Isaac and Larry entered his office. 'I'm innocent of any crime. If I didn't know better, I'd say this was victimisation.'

'It's not. Mr Knox, how are you with weapons?'

'What do you mean?'

'Can you fire a gun?'

'I was in the army, corporal. I know how to shoot. Does that make me a murderer? If it does, there are plenty of others with weapons training.'

'We're not interested in any others, only you. Did you visit a prostitute by the name of Gwendoline last night?'

'Why would I? This place is awash with willing females.'

'You told us last time that you'd upgraded the women, and they weren't available, not even to you.'

'Even so, a prostitute. Look at me, a man in the prime of life. Why would I go paying a woman for something I can get for free?'

'Can you?' Isaac said. 'There's not many women who'd like the manager of a strip club, let alone a murderer.'

'Are you accusing me?'

'Slater and his receptionist.'

'What about them?' Knox said. Both of the police officers looked for signs of nervousness in the man.

'Can I use your toilet?' Larry said.

'There's one out in the club.'

'There's one in here.'

'It's not working, doesn't flush properly.'

Larry ignored the man and opened the door to Knox's private bathroom. Inside he found a shower, a sink, and a toilet. He opened the cabinet above the sink. He then returned to where Isaac and Knox were. 'How long have you been using aftershave?' he said.

'Not often. Supposedly the one you saw in there is full of pheromones, drives the women wild.'

'Does it?'

'It's just advertising.'

'The man who used the services of a prostitute last night – the woman was a friend of Daisy, a flatmate of another murdered woman, and she remembers the smell of your aftershave. You were also with her on the night Helen Langdon and James Holden were murdered. Mr Knox, I put it to you that you are the murderer of Helen Langdon, James Holden, Daisy and another prostitute.'

'I've killed no one. I'm innocent,' Knox protested.

'Who paid you? Was it Archie Adamant? We know his father was involved with this club. We know that Aberman was killed on his instruction. Are you willing to go to jail without telling us the truth? Adamant, we can't pin anything on him. We need your testimony.'

Isaac knew that Homicide had enough to arrest Knox, not enough to ensure a conviction. Geraldine would prove to be an unreliable witness, and the smell of an aftershave that was not difficult to purchase would not convict the man.

'Mr Knox, with your testimony, we will arrest Archie Adamant.'

'He's not the father.'

'What does that mean?'

'Gerald Adamant, there was a real bastard, fooled everyone, even me.'

'Was he the person who gave the instruction for Aberman to be killed by Ugly Pete?'

'Gus told me. Adamant was a secretive man. Aberman, he's got the dirt on him, using it as leverage against the money owing. I didn't know, not for a long time, and then Gus, he's in a strange mood, wants to talk.'

'He told you?'

'He told me about that night. He and Ugly Pete had worked Ben Aberman over, Ugly Pete cranking the handle of the generator. Gus, he can be soft sometimes. He goes into the other room, disturbed by the smell of the burning flesh, Aberman arching off the chair. Five minutes later, Ugly Pete comes out and tells him it's all over.'

'What's all over?'

'Aberman, he's signed all the documents. Gus checks on the man. He's tied to the chair, his head flopped forward. Gus walks around to the front, sees the bullet hole.'

'A gun would have made a noise.'

'It had a silencer.'

'He would have heard something.'

'Gus's hearing is not great. He may not have heard.'

'Gus has admitted to burying Aberman. Why are you telling us?' Isaac said.

'I'm protecting myself. Gerald Adamant was the man behind the scenes. He was more dangerous than anyone else. A man devoid of any emotion, other than self-aggrandisement. What people thought of him was all-important.'

'And his son, Archie?'

'I'll not testify against him.'

'In that case, you'll go to jail for the murders of six people.'

'You can't prove it,' Knox said. Isaac and Larry could see that the man was rattled. Isaac knew that if he played Knox off against Adamant, one of them would break.

'Mr Knox, I'm arresting you for the murders of Helen Langdon and James Holden.'

'I've got a club to run. I don't have time for this.'

'Your doorman, he can deal with it. Larry, get the crime scene examiners over here and at Knox's home. You can check as well, see if you can find any weapons. Mr Knox shot Slater and his receptionist, also Daisy and Geraldine's flatmate. We need the weapon.'

Chapter 27

Barry Knox lived better than Larry had expected. He had a three-bedroom flat on the other side of the River Thames, in Greenwich, not far from the Greenwich Meridian, the line of zero degrees longitude.

Gordon Windsor's crime scene examiners were already on the site. The CSEs focussed on any evidence that would tie in Knox to any of the murder sites. Difficult, considering that very little had been found at any of them, bar the occasional hair, the lint from a piece of fabric. With the CSEs in one room, Larry moved carefully around the flat. There was no sign of a woman being resident, although the place was tidy. Realising that the CSEs would focus on the more obvious, Larry looked for hidden areas, loose tiles, a floorboard that creaked. After thirty minutes he hadn't found anything. He was preparing to leave when above him, just close to the front door, he saw an area of fresh paint. He called over Grant Meston, Windsor's deputy. 'What do you reckon to this?' Larry said.

Meston took a step ladder the team had brought with them. He climbed the three steps and tapped on the area. 'It sounds hollow,' he said.

Larry phoned Isaac. 'Keep Knox on ice. We need fifteen minutes.'

Meston took photos of the area before carefully using a sharp knife to find a crack. 'Here it is,' he said. Gingerly, he continued until he had removed a small square of plasterboard. Inside, a cavity with a package wedged in tight.

More photos and then the package was removed. It was placed on the table in the kitchen and slowly unwrapped. Inside was a gun with a silencer. 'It's the correct calibre, Glock 17, 9 mm,' Meston said.

'Can you confirm it's the murder weapon?'

'Not here. It'll need Forensics.'

Larry phoned Isaac once again. 'We've found a weapon. Forensics will check it out.'

Isaac turned to Knox who was waiting for his lawyer to arrive. 'Detective Inspector Hill has found a gun at your flat.'

'It's for protection.'

'Hidden behind a painted area in your flat? It'll be a couple of hours before Forensics confirms it as a murder weapon, long enough for your lawyer to try and save your arse.'

***

Archie Adamant was panicking. The doorman he had installed at Dixey's after Gus's arrest had phoned him: Barry Knox was in police custody, charged with murder.

Archie knew he did not have his father's natural ways with people and most had found him to be rude and boorish. However, he did have an innate ability to survive. He visited his sister in her part of the substantial home. 'Helen murdered our father. I found out some months ago.'

'How?'

'She had told Holden. He told me.'

'Why?'

'I knew the man. He thought I was the same as my father, full of magnanimity.'

'But why would she tell Holden? She had convinced everyone of her innocence.'

'According to Holden, she was in love. She did not want her present jeopardised by lying to the man.'

'But why did he tell you?'

'He thought he could trust me. He had trusted our father.'

'Holden was a naïve man. Did you kill him?' Abigail asked.

'Do you think I'm capable?'

'Capable enough to find someone to do it for you.'

'She murdered our father,' Archie said.

'Our father was becoming old and irrational. He could have written us out of his will at any time. Does Howard know about Helen?'

'What does he matter? He's only the spawn of that gold-digging woman that our father married.'

'And Slater, what about him? What did he know?'

'He knew too much for too long.'

'Did you kill him? You're a good shot.'

'You know the Adamant motto,' Archie said.

'Unwritten, but our father taught us well: get others to do your dirty work, and for you, an Adamant, to bask in the glory of piety.'

'They've arrested Barry Knox, the manager at Dixey's.'

'Did he kill Helen?'

'Yes.'

'On your authority?'

'I had no option. If Holden knew the truth, so would others. Helen was committed to telling all, and with it would come the checking, and questions about why she had killed our father. I had to do what was necessary.'

'And now?'

'I'm leaving the country. Knox knows too much, and he'll talk. I've arranged a private plane. Do you want to come?'

'I've not done anything wrong.'

Ten minutes later, Archie Adamant attempted to pull out of the driveway, only to find it blocked by two police cars. Quickly, he was bundled into one of the vehicles, his hands cuffed.

'Where are we going?' Adamant said.

'Challis Street Police Station. Detective Chief Inspector Isaac Cook has some questions for you.'

A plane waited at a nearby airport for a passenger who would never come.

***

Archie Adamant did not enjoy the trip to Challis Street Police Station, that was plain to see on his arrival. 'You'll regret this,' he said to Isaac when they met.

'Mr Adamant, we needed to act with urgency. Certain information has come into our possession which identifies you as a person of interest.' Isaac felt no need to say any more. Adamant had a Queen's Counsel coming to the office to represent him. Barry Knox, without the financial resources of the other man, had only a local lawyer.

In the first interview room sat Barry Knox; in the second, Archie Adamant. Outside, in the police station's reception area, were Abigail and Howard Adamant. 'You can't believe our brother is guilty of such crimes,' Abigail said.

'The proof is there. We can prove who killed Helen and James Holden, also the flatmate of one of the prostitutes. They link back to your brother. It's up to him to convince us otherwise.'

Barry Knox waited impatiently. He regretted hiding the gun in his flat, realising that he should have dumped it in the river not far from where he lived. He had always been reluctant to throw anything away, including old magazines and old newspapers, and now it was going to haunt him.

Isaac and Larry entered Interview Room 1. Across from them, Barry Knox and his lawyer. Isaac informed Knox of his rights, the procedure that would be followed during the interview. Knox nodded his head weakly; his lawyer too. Neither of the two police officers believed the lawyer would be able to achieve much.

'Mr Knox, the weapon discovered hidden in your flat has been positively identified as being used to kill Helen Langdon and James Holden. It has also been used to kill another woman.'

'I didn't kill anyone,' Knox said.

'The weapon's in your flat. It's hidden in a cavity in the wall, and the area concealed and painted over.'

'I didn't put it there.'

'Your fingerprints are on the paintbrush that our crime scene examiners found in the laundry. Your continual denial does you no credit. We have sufficient proof for a conviction.'

'Are my client's fingerprints on the gun?' the lawyer said.

'No. The gun is clean,' Isaac said.

'Then you only have circumstantial evidence, not proof.'

'No jury will accept that Mr Knox did not know the gun was in his flat, sealed behind a false façade, his fingerprints on the paintbrush, a pot of paint as well.'

'My client will maintain his innocence.'

'If that is what he wants. We've Archie Adamant in the other room. No doubt he'll be more than happy to blame someone else.'

'Mr Knox, why do you continue to deny this?' Larry said. He could see Knox wavering, wanting to indicate to his lawyer that he was ready to confess, the lawyer pressing on his client's arm to stay still and to let him deal with it.

'My client has no more to say.'

'He's guilty, we can prove it, and if he doesn't talk, then Adamant is going to place all the blame on him,' Isaac said.

'Very well, I killed Helen and Holden. I didn't want to, but Adamant, he was insistent,' Knox said.

'You could have refused.'

'I wanted to.'

'Then why?'

'Knox knew about my cheating him on the money the club was making. He threatened me with the Aberman solution.'

'You knew about Ben Aberman in the garden?'

'I knew he was dead. I was never sure where he was buried, although I suspected it was the garden. Gus said it was, but with him, I could never be certain.'

'Why weren't you certain?'

'Gus wasn't the brightest, and maybe Adamant had told him to tell me, a warning.'

'This is the older Adamant?'

'Yes, Gerald. He was a tough bastard. Always nice to your face, the sort of man who'd help old ladies across the road. But the man had an evil side. He'd have enjoyed watching Aberman suffer, and then Ugly Pete shooting him in the head.'

'Were you there?'

'Not me. I didn't have anything to do with Aberman's death.'

'Tell us about Archie Adamant.'

'He's worse than the father. Gerald was likeable, but the son's not. The son, he phoned me up, tells me that that Helen had murdered his father in cold blood. He wants revenge.'

'Did he care that much about the father?'

'Archie, I doubt it.'

'How do you know all this?'

'A week after Aberman died, Helen phoned me up. She had left the club by then. We met a few days later.'

'You've known all these years?'

'Not all of it, but over the years other bits of information have fallen into place. Helen, she's confused, not sure what to do. We meet over a few weeks, formulate this plan.'

'The death of Gerald Adamant?'

'Helen, she's a great actor. She knew she'd need to get close to the man, to make him suffer for what he had done.'

'Did she love Aberman?'

'He treated her well.'

'Why did she phone you?'

'You don't get it, do you? Aberman's dead, Helen's still alive and so am I. Neither of us doubts that Gerald Adamant is capable of arranging someone's death. We start spending more time together, end up sharing a bed. After a couple of months, the heat goes out of the romance.'

'Romance?'

'Not the best word,' Knox said. 'We're thrown together by a mutual problem. There's no one else we can confide in, and don't say the police. If we had told you, we'd still be on the street, and Adamant would have dealt with us. The original plan wasn't to kill Gerald Adamant, only to discredit him, expose him for what he was.'

'What changed?'

'Helen saw beneath the veneer. She realised that if he knew he had been engineered into marriage, he would react. She

'It's in the records. He was starting to get old, he had a medical condition, and he didn't like it. Helen was there for him to deny the ageing process.'

'Did he marry her for love or for lust?'

'Both. None of us objected.'

'You did at first.'

'We didn't know who she was, although our father was smitten, more so than he had been with any woman for a long time.'

'You must have known her history.'

'Not then, and out of respect for our father, we did not hire private investigators to check.'

'Why? A woman, young and provocative, entered into your house. Aren't you suspicious?'

'We were, but we're not a poor family. If he wanted to squander some of his money on her, it did not concern us, as long as she made him happy.'

'Did she?'

'Yes, but this is well known. She proved to be the ideal wife, loving and caring, devoted to the causes he held dear to his heart.'

'This is all very well,' the QC said, 'but why is my client here, and why the handcuffs? He's not been charged with any crime.'

'We had been forewarned that Mr Adamant was about to leave the country. In fact, there was a plane waiting for him not more than ten miles from his house.'

'Is that an issue?' Adamant said.

'Not in itself, but the flight plan had been lodged at the last moment, and it was an executive jet on hire to you.'

'I often use executive jets.'

'We will be checking the financial records of your businesses and those of the charitable trust. Will we find any anomalies?'

'No.'

'We will also be questioning your brother and sister. Will they corroborate your story?'

'They will, although Howard, he doesn't want to become involved, and Abigail, she's not interested.'

'We've arrested two men in connection with the death of Ben Aberman. One of those men will state that your father gave the order for his murder.'

'I don't believe it. My father was a good man who helped others.'

'He was not there when it happened. He was a man who controlled from a distance. Are you such a man?'

'No. I have taken over my father's interests, business and charitable, that's all.'

'Successfully?'

'Not as successfully as my father, but both are sound.'

'Why not?'

'My father was a unique individual. People instinctively liked and trusted him. I do not have the ready ease he had. It's my personality, and I can't change it. I can only do what I feel is best for the Adamant family.'

'Even if that includes murder?'

'I must object,' Westfield said. 'You are not accusing my client of any crime, only questioning him. Where's the proof that he's done anything criminal?'

'There are enough bodies. Mr Adamant is not the person, nor was his father, to commit any act of violence personally. That is always left to others. We can put forward a strong case showing that Gerald Adamant was behind the death of Ben Aberman. We can also show that Helen Langdon was aware of who killed Aberman and that she executed a plan to marry your father, and to ultimately kill him.'

'That's rubbish. You never saw the two of them together. I did. Helen loved my father. The verdict against her at the trial was erroneous. All three of us knew it, but they dragged up her past history, and she was damned.'

'My client is not here to answer questions regarding his father,' Westfield said.

'We have a statement from Barry Knox, a man who has admitted to killing Helen Langdon, James Holden, and two prostitutes. He has stated that you were the person behind the scenes, giving the orders.'

'For two prostitutes? What for?'

'They're collateral damage. One of them had figured out what was going on, and the flatmate of the other woman had identified Knox as the murderer. We can prove his guilt, and he has given us a full confession. Mr Adamant, yours is not so easy. You've inherited the skill of staying out of sight from your father,' Isaac said. 'Both Detective Inspector Hill and I were in Slater's office when he and his receptionist were killed. Knox did not commit those murders, although you, Mr Adamant, are a good shot. Did you kill Slater, realising that he was getting scared, or he was the only one who could positively identify you?'

'Objection,' Westfield said. 'This is conjecture, not proof.'

'We will obtain the proof. There is enough evidence to overturn Helen Langdon's acquittal. It will show her guilty of the murder of the man who ordered Ben Aberman's death. We can also prove that Slater was at Aberman's house when he signed the documents ceding his clubs to a company associated with your father. Mr Adamant, your defence is based on your father's reputation. Within the next few months, that reputation will be shattered.'

'It's a tragedy what you are doing. My father helped a lot of people around the world.'

'And that excuses him from prosecution?'

'No, but you are wrong, and as Westfield said, it's conjecture, not proof.'

'A father's reputation destroyed, even if you can prove it, does not alter the fact that a person is innocent until proven guilty,' Westfield said.

'The lofty pedestal of the father will be destroyed. It will be more difficult to prove that innocence, and we will have Knox accusing your client.'

'Is that it?' Westfield said.

'For the present,' Isaac said. 'There is one other issue. We will be conducting a thorough search of the Adamant family home and its surroundings.'

'For what?' Adamant said. 'This farce has gone on long enough.'

'Knox did not kill Slater and his receptionist; however, you, Mr Adamant, are a crack shot. We have records of you competing in various competitions in this country.'

'I would request time to confer with my client,' Westfield said.

Isaac adjourned the interview.

'What do you reckon?' Goddard asked outside the interview room.

'Guilt by association, that's all,' Isaac said. The three police officers were taking the opportunity to discuss the case.

'We need his conviction,' Goddard said. 'Any chance of an arrest?'

'We can hold him based on Knox's statement. The proof is up to others.'

The interview resumed, Adamant looking more at ease. His QC leant forward over the table. It was meant to intimidate; it did not work. 'My client wishes to make a statement,' he said.

Adamant cleared his throat. 'I, Archibald Adamant, am not responsible for the accusations levelled against me. My father, Gerald Adamant, a respected member of society, did, at all times, conduct his business affairs in accordance with the laws of this country. He has committed no crime. If he purchased certain clubs, they would have been part of a portfolio, as my father had no interest in places of disrepute. His wife, Helen, was a woman of good character, who myself, Abigail, my sister, and Howard, my younger brother, held in the highest esteem. The charges levelled against her were spurious and took her past lifestyle into account. She loved my father, he loved her. She acted in self-defence and served four years in jail before being acquitted. That acquittal was due to the efforts of James Holden, a believer in the rights of the poor and downtrodden. He arranged her release from jail, the overturning of the original conviction, and her rehabilitation into society.

'The fact that she was in a hotel room with the man when they were both violently murdered does not impact on our fondness for the woman. Why she and James Holden were killed is unknown to me. I was not responsible for issuing a directive to Barry Knox, the manager of the Dixey Club. I knew the man, as I also knew Slater.

'Barry Knox was, and still is, a character of disrepute. I know he had been using the club for prostitution as well as for the sale of drugs. Helen knew this as well, a possible reason for Knox to kill her. I was arrested and brought here in handcuffs. I object to this, and a formal complaint will be lodged. At no time was I planning to leave this country on a permanent basis, and I, as a free citizen, am able to choose my mode of transport as befits my status and my finances. I maintain that I am innocent of any charges levelled against me.'

'Thank you, Mr Adamant,' Isaac said. 'Due to the seriousness of the charges, you will be held while further investigations are conducted.'

Chapter 29

'Not a good interview,' Larry said outside the interview room. 'A disaster,' Isaac said. 'The man's right, our evidence is flimsy, more assumption than fact.'

'You've got thirty-six hours to fix this up, or else Adamant is out of here, and his QC is going to raise the roof,' Goddard said.

Isaac realised he had been premature in bringing Adamant into the station, but there had been no option with the man's impending departure from the country. There was no doubt that he was guilty, but without proof the case against him was going nowhere. Isaac realised that, once again, time was of the essence. He phoned Bridget. 'Fifteen minutes, everyone in the office.'

'Tough day, sir,' Bridget said. She had sensed the frustration in Isaac's voice.

'You're a bit of a hero down at Scotland Yard,' Goddard said after Isaac had ended his call. 'Davies is singing your praises after you wrapped up five murders. Don't stuff it up.'

'Archie Adamant, he's tough. We'll not break him easily,' Isaac said.

'He's got public opinion behind him. Anything other than cast-iron proof is not going to hold up.'

'We'll come up with the proof. The team won't let me down.'

In Homicide, the team sat down. No one would be going home until all avenues had been explored.

'What do we have against Archie Adamant?' Isaac said. 'Apart from Knox and Aberman's ex-wife, do we have anyone else?'

'Gus, the Dixey Club's doorman, and Ugly Pete?'

'Gus had no dealings with the man, and Ugly Pete is a murderer. It will need something decisive and indisputable to ensure a conviction.'

'Abigail Adamant, what do we reckon to her?' Larry said.

'Frivolous, interested in a good time,' Wendy said.

'If Adamant goes down for murder, it's her lifestyle that will be curtailed. She'd not want that,' Isaac said.

'We were there when Slater was shot. He was about to tell us something,' Larry said.

'But why? Whatever he said would have only been to protect himself, place the blame on others. Or maybe he was frightened for his life. Whoever shot him had panicked and seen the danger.'

'Self-protection?'

'Has Slater's office been checked, his clients' files?'

'The man was meticulous,' Bridget said. 'Fraud checked, found nothing untoward. The papers for Aberman's house were there.'

'Wendy, spend time with Aberman's neighbour. Larry and I will stay here with Bridget, see what else we can find,' Isaac said.

***

Wendy found Mrs Hawthorne in a good mood. 'It's her next door.'

'What about her?' Wendy asked.

'Her husband was here last night. They had a terrible argument. I could hear it from my side of the fence.'

Wendy knew that Mrs Hawthorne was just the sort of person a murder investigation needs; the last thing a neighbour wants.

'What was said?'

'I wasn't listening, not particularly.' Wendy knew she was.

'Maybe if we sit down and have a cup of tea,' Wendy suggested.

Knox was languishing in prison, awaiting trial. Adamant was being held at Challis Street, and he was about to walk free, which would only mean trouble. Already the man's QC had been on the phone to DCS Goddard and to Commissioner Davies.

'I only hope you know what you're doing,' Goddard commented to Isaac after he had ended the call from the QC.

Davies's reaction had been more direct. 'Don't let Cook stuff this up.' So much for the honeymoon period, Goddard thought after the commissioner ended the call.

'Mrs Hawthorne, what was the argument about?' Wendy said. Both of the women were sitting comfortably by an imitation wood fire. Wendy was anxious to draw the information out of a woman who was glad of the company.

'She wanted him to stay at the house, he didn't. Something about it being a shrine to a dead man, a man she loved more than him.'

'Is that all?'

'The husband's right. The woman, she fusses around where Mr Aberman's body was found, even erected a little cross.'

Wendy realised the woman didn't only look over the fence, she also had a pair of binoculars. She could sympathise with Aberman's ex-wife.

'What happened with the husband? Did he stay?'

'Not him. He slammed the door hard on his way out and got into his car.'

'The woman?'

'I didn't see her again. She had a visitor later.'

'Do you know who it was?'

'It was Archie.'

'Archie Adamant?' Wendy said. The name had come as a surprise to her. 'I didn't know you knew the Adamants.'

'I don't, not really. Before I retired, I was a teacher at a school not far from here. Very expensive, it was. It was Archie, I'm certain, even though it was twenty, maybe twenty-five years ago. Back then, he was skinny, used to play football for the school team. Now, he's overweight, and not very attractive.'

'How can you be certain?'

'I always remember my boys. He was a little surly, a bully sometimes, but his academic results were fine, and he was a fine sportsman.'

'We've arrested Archie Adamant for murder,' Wendy said.

'I'm not surprised.'

'Why?'

'I knew his father was successful, although I never met him. The mother would come sometimes, but she died. After that, Archie seemed to spend a lot of time on his own. He used to cheat in the exams.'

'Did you catch him?'

'I saw him do it once, told him I'd report him the next time.'

'Did he stop?'

'Archie? I doubt it, just became more careful. He was always pushing the boundaries.'

'Sneaking young girls into the school? I'm assuming it was boarding.'

'It was, but not Archie. Some of the other boys did. I don't know why as he wasn't a bad-looking boy.'

'He's never married,' Wendy said.

'He wasn't gay, or at least, I don't think he was.'

'He wasn't. The man is celibate. What else can you tell me about him?'

'Not much more. I continued for a few years more at the school before retiring. Last night was the first time I'd seen him since.'

Wendy made a phone call to Isaac. 'Archie Adamant's been out to Aberman's house, met with the man's widow.'

'Give me thirty-five minutes, and we'll go and interview her. Is she at home?'

'There's a car in the driveway.'

Wendy turned to Mrs Hawthorne. 'Is she there?'

'She's not been out.'

'She's in the house,' Wendy said to Isaac.

'Make sure she doesn't leave.'

'I'll put my car in her driveway, block her exit.'

'That'll do.'

'The missing piece?' Wendy said.

'I hope so.'

***

Isaac, acutely conscious of the remaining time he could hold Adamant in custody at Challis Street, made the trip to Bray in thirty-two minutes. 'Does she know we're here?' Isaac asked.

'I'm sure she does,' Wendy said.

The two police officers walked down the driveway of Aberman's old house. Wendy knocked on the door.

'Sergeant Gladstone, what do you want?'

'I'm here with DCI Cook. We've a few questions for you.'

'Very well, do come in.'

The three sat in the kitchen. 'It's the warmest place in the house,' the woman said. Wendy thought she was remarkably calm, as if she was making an effort to conceal her true feelings.

'Last night you had a visitor,' Wendy said.

'I had two. My husband, although he did not stay long.'

'Why's that?'

'It's her next door, isn't it?'

'What happened last night should concern you more.'

'My husband has become difficult. He wants to live in London, I want to live here.'

'Is that it?'

'He thinks I'm becoming obsessive about the house, as if it's become a remembrance of Ben.'

'Has it?'

'I can't help remembering the good times we had here, it's only natural, and I certainly don't believe the spirit of the dead man walks the house at night.'

'The room where he died?' Isaac asked.

'My husband planned to make it into a study. If he doesn't want to come here, then I'll find a use for it.'

'Will he come?'

'What option does he have? Both of the houses are in my name. If he wants London, then he can find himself a bedsit.'

'Do you want him to come here?'

'It's up to him. I like it here. He's no Ben, just a man for the cold nights.'

'I've not heard you speak like that before,' Wendy said.

'I'm angry. He's a decent man even if he can be tiresome at times. He'll come, and I'll be glad of his company.'

'Your other visitor interests us more,' Isaac said. 'Archie Adamant.'

'Had you met him before?'

'It was the first time.'

'What did he say?'

'He threatened me. He told me if I said anything it would not be good for me.'

'Should we reconvene at Challis Street Police Station? Do you need legal representation?' Wendy said.

'Why? I've done nothing wrong.'

'On the contrary. We've suspected you for some time. Of all those involved with your husband and his death, you are the only one who has emerged unscathed,' Isaac said. 'Helen Langdon died for what she was going to tell. Slater died for what he knew, and two prostitutes died because they could recognise the murderer, yet you have remained comfortably cocooned.'

'I've nothing to feel guilty about. I was married to a man who became involved with unscrupulous people. It cost him his life.'

'Why did this house remain in your name for all those years, yet it was Helen who looked after the place? Were you party to a conspiracy to conceal the truth? Did you know that your husband was to be killed? And why Archie Adamant?'

'I've told you. He knocked on the door, pushed his way in and threatened me.'

'Threatened you with what? If you're innocent, now is the time to tell us the truth. Archie Adamant is under lock and key. He can do nothing to you at this time.'

'He controls from afar.'

'He controlled through Slater. Barry Knox was the instrument that killed. Both of them can no longer concern you. It is just the police you need to worry about. If you're not forthcoming, we will need to take you to Challis Street and charge you with withholding information. Do you want that?'

'No. I knew my husband had died, not long after his death.'

'Helen phoned you?'

'She told me what had happened and that she had managed to convince Gerald Adamant to leave her with the house to look after.'

'What did you say?'

'What could I say? My husband had fallen foul of people who solved their problems by murder. I didn't want to be another statistic. My life was more precious than that.'

'Your husband?'

'I was sad, but I knew he lived on the edge. His death did not come as a surprise, and we were divorced by then.'

'And you remained in his will as his heir.'

'Ben was a good man, don't let anyone else tell you differently. We were on speaking terms, and there was no bitterness. He wanted his life, I wanted mine. I stayed in Chelsea, and he signed the house over to me. I preferred this house in the country, but he wanted the parties. We agreed, and I always remained in his will.'

'After the divorce, did you see him very much?'

'Rarely, but sometimes we'd meet for a couple of hours.'

'Why did Archie threaten you when everyone else has died? Were you involved with Archie Adamant's father?'

'It was a long time ago. I was divorced, he was on his own.'

'Were you with him when your husband died?'

'Yes. When I heard what had happened, I knew it was Gerald. He never discussed what he did, although I knew. He was a charismatic man, as was Ben. I loved them both, but after what had happened, I left Gerald and found myself a boringly honest man.'

'Do you regret it?'

'I regret nothing. I don't regret Ben or Gerald, and I don't regret marrying a bank manager. Life is what you make of it. Regret for past mistakes and lost opportunities count for nothing.'

'Are you willing to testify against Archie Adamant?'

'What for? What do I know?'

'You know everything,' Isaac said. 'You're playing us for suckers. We've heard about the cross in the garden for your first husband. Is that an act of redemption, to appease your guilt over his death? Did you set up the deal with Adamant to ensure the house would stay with you?'

'No, yes, I don't know.' Wendy knew that Isaac was maintaining the pressure, waiting for the woman to falter.

'Christine Aberman, you've been there all along. Gerald Adamant was smart, staying out of sight, acting as a benefactor of the downtrodden, the weak, the impoverished. And there you are, in league with the man. When did you find out about Helen and Holden?'

'She phoned Knox, Archie told me last night. It was Archie's idea to remove Helen as a threat; he confided in me.'

'Why?'

'His family's name.'

'Slater?'

'That was Archie. You were in his office, and Slater knows what's going on. The police are close to uncovering the truth. Slater's made plenty of money from the Adamants over the years, but he's ready to distance himself, to claim that he was acting on instructions.'

'But he was at the house when Ben Aberman was killed.'

'It was becoming too complicated. Archie was planning to make a run for it. I'm staying here, maintaining a low profile.'

'Why did Archie trust you? Why did Gerald?'

'They both knew a kindred spirit. Archie, he was fond of me, even when I was with his father. He's got this problem, but he could talk to me about it. I was a sympathetic ear, and the Adamants, whatever else they may be, are loyal.'

'You're not loyal to them now?'

'Archie would have turned against me in time. Maybe not this year, but sometime. I'm stopping it now.'

'Will you give us a written statement? Will you testify?'

'Yes. I've killed no one, and the houses are still mine.'

'You won't be seeing them for a long time,' Wendy said.

'A long time, but I will see them one day. That's all that matters. The future, like the past, holds no fears for me.'

Isaac phoned Larry. 'We have the whole story. How did you get on with the gun that killed Slater and his receptionist?'

'We dug up the vegetable patch at Adamant's house. We found a rifle.'

'Forensics?'

'They're checking now. It's the right calibre.'

'How did you know where to look?'

'Instinct. I just thought where I'd hide it.'

'Have you spoken to Adamant?'

'He's admitted to his guilt.'

Isaac phoned Detective Chief Superintendent Goddard who called Commissioner Alwyn Davies. Davies was delighted, singing the praises of the best detective chief inspector in the London Metropolitan Police. Isaac knew he did not mean it.

The End

ALSO BY THE AUTHOR

Death at Coombe Farm – A DI Tremayne Thriller

A warring family. A disputed inheritance. A recipe for death.

If it hadn't been for the circumstances, Detective Inspector Keith Tremayne would have said the view was outstanding. Up high, overlooking the farmhouse in the valley below, the panoramic vista of Salisbury Plain stretching out beyond.

The only problem was that near where he stood with his sergeant, Clare Yarwood, there was a body, and it wasn't a pleasant sight.

Death and the Lucky Man – A DI Tremayne Thriller

Sixty-eight million pounds and dead.

Hardly the outcome expected for the luckiest man in England the day his lottery ticket was drawn out of the barrel.

But then, Alan Winters' rags-to-riches story had never been conventional, and there were those who had benefited, but others who hadn't.

Death and the Assassin's Blade – A DI Tremayne Thriller

It was meant to be high drama, not murder, but someone's switched the daggers. The man's death took place in plain view of two serving police officers.

He was not meant to die; the daggers were only theatrical props, plastic and harmless. A summer's night, a production of Julius Caesar amongst the ruins of an Anglo-Saxon fort. Detective Inspector Tremayne is there with his sergeant, Clare Yarwood. In the assassination scene, Caesar collapses to the ground. Brutus defends his actions; Mark Antony rebukes him.

They're a disparate group, the amateur actors. One's an estate agent, another an accountant. And then there is the teenage school student, the gay man, the funeral director. And what about the women? They could be involved.

They've each got a secret, but which of those on the stage wanted Gordon Mason, the actor who had portrayed Caesar, dead?

Murder is the Only Option – A DCI Cook Thriller

A man, thought to be long dead, returns to exact revenge against those who had blighted his life. His only concern is to protect his wife and daughter. He will stop at nothing to achieve his aim.

'Big Greg, I never expected to see you around here at this time of night.'

'I've told you enough times.'

'I've no idea what you're talking about,' Robertson replied. He looked up at the man, only to see a metal pole coming down at him. Robertson fell down, cracking his head against a concrete kerb.

The two vagrants, no more than twenty feet away, did not stir and did not even look in the direction of the noise. If they had, they would have seen a dead body, another man walking away.

Death Unholy – A DI Tremayne Thriller

All that remained were the man's two legs and a chair full of greasy and fetid ash. Little did DI Keith Tremayne know that it was the beginning of a journey into the murky world of paganism and its ancient rituals. And it was going to get very dangerous.

'Do you believe in spontaneous human combustion?' Detective Inspector Keith Tremayne asked.

'Not me. I've read about it. Who hasn't?' Sergeant Clare Yarwood answered.

I haven't,' Tremayne replied, which did not surprise his young sergeant. In the months they had been working together, she had come to realise that he was a man who had little interest in the world. When he had a cigarette in his mouth, a beer in his hand, and a murder to solve he was about the happiest she ever saw him. He could hardly be regarded as one of life's sociable people. And as for reading? The most he managed was an occasional police report or an early morning newspaper, turning first to the back pages for the racing results.

Murder in Little Venice – A DCI Cook Thriller

A dismembered corpse floats in the canal in Little Venice, an upmarket tourist haven in London. Its identity is unknown, but what is its significance?

DCI Isaac Cook is baffled about why it's there. Is it gang-related, or is it something more?

Whatever the reason, it's clearly a warning, and Isaac and his team are sure it's not the last body that they'll have to deal with.

Murder is only a Number – A DCI Cook Thriller

Before she left she carved a number in blood on his chest. But why the number 2, if this was her first murder?

The woman prowls the streets of London. Her targets are men who have wronged her. Or have they? And why is she keeping count?

DCI Cook and his team finally know who she is, but not before she's murdered four men. The whole team are looking for her, but the woman keeps disappearing in plain sight. The pressure's on to stop her, but she's always one step ahead.

And this time, DCS Goddard can't protect his protégé, Isaac Cook, from the wrath of the new commissioner at the Met.

Murder House – A DCI Cook Thriller

A corpse in the fireplace of an old house. It's been there for thirty years, but who is it?

It's clearly murder, but who is the victim and what connection does the body have to the previous owners of the house. What is the motive? And why is the body in a fireplace? It was bound to be discovered eventually but was that what the murderer wanted? The main suspects are all old and dying, or already dead.

Isaac Cook and his team have their work cut out trying to put the pieces together. Those who know are not talking because of an old-fashioned belief that a family's dirty laundry should not be aired in public, and certainly not to a policeman – even if that means the murderer is never brought to justice!

Murder is a Tricky Business – A DCI Cook Thriller

A television actress is missing, and DCI Isaac Cook, the Senior Investigation Officer of the Murder Investigation Team at Challis Street Police Station in London, is searching for her.

Why has he been taken away from more important crimes to search for the woman? It's not the first time she's gone missing, so why does everyone assume she's been murdered?

There's a secret, that much is certain, but who knows it? The missing woman? The executive producer? His eavesdropping assistant? Or the actor who portrayed her fictional brother in the TV soap opera?

Murder Without Reason – A DCI Cook Thriller

DCI Cook faces his greatest challenge. The Islamic State is waging war in England, and they are winning.

Not only does Isaac Cook have to contend with finding the perpetrators, but he is also being forced to commit actions contrary to his mandate as a police officer.

And then there is Anne Argento, the prime minister's deputy. The prime minister has shown himself to be a pacifist and is not up to the task. She needs to take his job if the country is to fight back against the Islamists.

Vane and Martin have provided the solution. Will DCI Cook and Anne Argento be willing to follow it through? Are they able to act for the good of England, knowing that a criminal and murderous action is about to take place? Do they have any option?

The Haberman Virus

A remote and isolated village in the Hindu Kush mountain range in North Eastern Afghanistan is wiped out by a virus unlike any seen before.

A mysterious visitor clad in a space suit checks his handiwork, a female American doctor succumbs to the disease, and the woman sent to trap the person responsible falls in love with him – the man who would cause the deaths of millions.

Hostage of Islam

Three are to die at the Mission in Nigeria: the pastor and his wife in a blazing chapel; another gunned down while trying to defend them from the Islamist fighters.

Kate McDonald, an American, grieving over her boyfriend's death and Helen Campbell, whose life had been troubled by drugs and prostitution, are taken by the attackers.

Kate is sold to a slave trader who intends to sell her virginity to an Arab Prince. Helen, to ensure their survival, gives herself to the murderer of her friends.

Malika's Revenge

Malika, a drug-addicted prostitute, waits in a smugglers' village for the next Afghan tribesman or Tajik gangster to pay her price, a few scraps of heroin.

Yusup Baroyev, a drug lord, enjoys a lifestyle many would envy. An Afghan warlord sees the resurgence of the Taliban. A Russian white-collar criminal portrays himself as a good and honest citizen in Moscow.

All of them are linked in an audacious plan to increase the quantity of heroin shipped out of Afghanistan and into Russia and ultimately the West.

Some will succeed, some will die, some will be rescued from their plight and others will rue the day they became involved.

ABOUT THE AUTHOR

Phillip Strang was born in England in the late forties, during the post-war baby boom.

An avid reader of science fiction in his teenage years: Isaac Asimov, Frank Herbert, the masters of the genre. Still an avid reader, the author now mainly reads thrillers.

In his early twenties, the author, with a degree in electronics engineering and a desire to see the world, left England for Sydney, Australia. Now, forty years later, he still resides in Australia, although many intervening years were spent in a myriad of countries, some calm and safe, others no more than war zones.

Printed in Great Britain
by Amazon

60639259R00142